S0-ABC-188

...AND THEN HE
SHOT HIS COUSIN

JEREMIAH COBRA

Copyright © 2020 Jeremiah Cobra

All rights reserved.

ISBN: 978-0-9999043-0-5

To the light that we all strive for…

LET US NOT SPEAK OF MURDER

One bullet into his chest. One glimpse of light into the darkness. One heart torn apart. What's funny is though Justice Rooks lay in that darkness, bleeding onto the street that was already shimmering wet from the rain, it was I who could not move. He did plenty of moving—heaving and writhing from the pain and all that. But I stood perfectly still, watching his blood and the rain turn the asphalt into a black river beneath the street lamps. I might have walked on this river, walked away on its currents of light. Instead, I could only stare into the darkness as police sirens wailed in the distance. I did not even lower the hand that held the gun that fired into my cousin's chest.

Perhaps I redeemed myself with that bullet. After all, what would have happened if I had not done what I did? Justice had wanted to rob Eula Mae Reeves. She was one of those church-going ladies who always had a smile, a hug, and a peppermint candy for kids when the sermons were most unbearably long. It was said that she counted her blessings a little too loudly, drove her red convertible too proudly, acted like the hood couldn't touch her. She was a little bougie sometimes. But that was no reason to rob her. It was certainly no reason to kill her. And Justice would have if she had come home before we could get out of her house... My God! How many lives had I saved?

Brea. I definitely saved her life. Justice had already harmed her earlier that night. There might have been harsher words for what he did to her, but it was hard to know which to use since she was his girl and all that. She was going to leave him, though. That night, in fact. She told me so. I'm not saying she was going to be with me instead. Only that she was going to leave him. And not that I wanted to be with her or anything like that. I just knew that Justice did not deserve her. He didn't appreciate her beauty or her spirit. It was more like he was just keeping everybody else from admiring her. He was selfish that way. He hated every dude that spoke more than two words to her. Except me. I didn't count.

"You're like one of her girlfriends," he once joked. "Ain't 'Stacey' a girl's name, anyway?"

He was right about that part—about Brea and me being friends. Since sophomore year in high school. She told me everything.

Justice cheated on her once.

Okay, more than once.

They had even fought once.

Okay, more than once.

She cried on my shoulder most Sunday afternoons— after they both had been at each other's throats the night before. But they always made up by Monday. That was her spirit. She didn't believe in evil people. "Just evil choices," as she put it. A good friend would have told her to leave him. But a guy can't say that to another man's girl. Not unless he's a bitch. And I ain't no bitch. Justice was wrong about that part. Stacey wasn't a girl's name. It was my name. And I ain't no bitch.

Sometimes, Brea did get the idea to leave him on her own. The last time she told me she was going to leave him was that night before Justice and I went to rob Eula Mae. She was certain that she was done with him. But when I talked to Justice, he spoke as if nothing had changed. Perhaps she had said "no." But Justice always got his way.

Not anymore, though. Not after I murdered him. No, let us not speak of murder. Not yet. Family may fight together. Family may even fight each other. But family ain't supposed to kill each other. And Justice was the only family I knew. I had known him almost my whole life. I could never murder him.

MY COUSIN'S KEEPER

"Just keep a look out!" Justice called out to me from the bedroom. I was in the living room. I peered through the curtains of a narrow window, past the iron bars, and toward an empty space in the parking lot. There were other empty spaces, but I was supposed to keep my eye on the one marked "#7" and be ready to signal Justice when a gray, 1988 Chevrolet Caprice pulled into it. I needed to focus. However, my mind was on the happenings of the bedroom. It was noisy in there. Too noisy. Was it supposed to be that loud? All kinds of squeaks and bangs. Wood scraping against wood. And music. Who would play music at a time like this? And rap music of all things? Of course, Justice would. He usually had something playing, and he had just bought a new cassette. I guess he needed a soundtrack to his life, and who told a story better than Tupac?

Me against the world...

The bass of the music rumbled the wall. Justice would never hear my signal, but maybe he didn't really care to. Justice wasn't afraid of anything, and he could bullshit his way into or out of anything. I hated watching him get away with his bullshit.

Maybe I won't even give the signal, I thought. *Maybe I'll just leave him in there to get caught. Let's see him talk his way out of that.*

Yet, I knew that I could not let Justice be caught. Our fates were tied; if he got caught, I got caught. We would both be in just as much trouble. My heart pounded with the music until it faded out. Then another song began.

How long was this supposed to take?

I shifted uneasily by the window. Then I saw the gray, boxy Chevy enter the parking lot. I ducked away from the window and sprang toward the wall. Drum lines thumped against it. I tried tapping out the signal that we had agreed upon, but even I had trouble hearing it. There was some kind of vocal utterance from behind the wall, but otherwise the music and noises continued. I tapped again and ran back to the window to peer through the curtain. There she was, closing the door to the Chevy and shuffling up the sidewalk to the building entrance. I ran back to the wall and rammed my shoulder against it twice. The music stopped. I could hear him scrambling about. There were no hiding places in that room, and she had to be coming up the hall now.

Keys jingled on the other side of the door.

"W-w-where she at?" Justice called from the bedroom.

"Shh!" I hissed. "She's almost at the door."

"D-d-don't let her in!" he said.

"How I'm s'posed to do that?" I asked. "It's her house! She'll know something's wrong."

"J-j-just do something. Buy me a few more minutes."

But it was too late. The key clicked into the lock.

Damn it!

I sprang toward the window, stumbling over shoes and collapsing onto the sofa where I closed my eyes and hoped I had not been heard. The front door opened. I opened my eyes just a peek, enough to see Mama Etta shuffle through it.

"Boy!" she called to me. "Get up from there and help me with these groceries."

I closed my eyes tightly and exhaled a loud, fake snore.

"Stop playing with me, boy!" she warned. "I know you ain't sleep. Get your lazy-ass up and help me with this food. And where's that knuckle-headed grandson of mine?"

I snorted and stretched on the couch.

"He sleep, too," I said, trying my best to sound drowsy. However, when I saw her turn toward his room, I jumped up.

"I'll get him," I said. "But you know how he is when he's sleep. Takes him a minute to snap out of it."

Mama Etta cut me a side-glance but rolled her eyes and shuffled into the kitchen. I sighed with relief, but my heart raced as I walked to Justice's bedroom door. I tapped lightly on it.

"Yo," I whispered. "You good?"

The doorknob clicked and he pulled the door ajar to whisper through the sliver of an opening.

"Where she at?" he asked.

"Kitchen."

He opened the door a little wider. I looked at the curtains flailing before the open window. Then I looked back to Justice. A wide and mischievous grin spread across his face.

6

"You did good," he said, wrapping his arm around my neck and locking my head in the crook of his elbow.

"Nigga!" I cried, "Get off me!"

He wrestled me to the floor.

"Take that punk beating," he laughed as I struggled to get out of his headlock. I hated when he went into wrestler mode, even if he was just pretending.

Goddamned, fake-ass, WCW bullshit, I thought. *You ain't Sid Justice. Just regular-ass Justice.*

There was no way to get him to stop. Only a voice from the kitchen could save me.

"Y'all hush up that noise!" Mama Etta called to us. "I don't wanna hear that ignorance in my house."

Justice released me then, and I was grateful that he had listened to his grandma. He didn't listen to many people, and even she often chastised him in vain. She was almost eighty years old; what could she do to him?

"Son of a bitch," I huffed. I looked again at the billowing curtains as I caught my breath. "You made her go out the window?"

"Same way she got in, ain't it?" he replied.

"Whatever. Let's get the groceries."

"You don't wanna hear how it went?"

"I heard all I needed to hear," I said. "Y'all was loud as hell."

His lips curled into one of those cocky half smiles of his. In earnest, I was curious. Kya was the prettiest girl in the neighborhood. And she was a junior. Upperclassman. Every teenage boy around here was curious about her, and not just because most of us were probably still virgins. I mean, I was definitely still a virgin. But, I didn't want to hear about her from Justice.

7

"Nah, I'm cool," I replied. "Let's get these groceries before Mama Etta gets mad. I already saved your ass once today."

"My hero, Stacey," Justice said, raising his hand to my head. However, I caught him before he could *son* me. It's funny how we all know the way that fathers sometimes pat the backs of their boys' heads when they want to show affection and pride. I knew this even though I didn't have a father. Neither did Justice. Neither did most of the boys around here. Yet "son" had become a common word: a term of endearment, a threat, or a warning. "Son" was a word to be taken for granted. Like "nigga."

What's good, son?

Back up, son!

You don't know me like that, son!

Sometimes, it was just a verb to us, a gesture of reverence or an act of superiority. It was this last, more common usage that made me hate when Justice tried to son me, and I pushed his hand away.

"Come on," he said. "Let's get these groceries so we can eat. A man like me gotta keep his strength up." He winked at me and sprang to his feet. Then he bounded from the room. The race was on. I sprang after him. Outside the apartment, we raced all the way down the hall. I nearly caught him at the metal doors that led outside, but he won this first contest, leaving me to secure the cement block that kept those doors from locking behind us.

At the trunk of the gray Chevy, we competed again to carry more bags than the other. I lost this contest, too and I watched Justice lumber back to the apartment.

8

This time, I cruised past him and he had to stop and ensure that both doors latched closed behind us. We laughed and boasted as we crashed through the apartment door. Mama Etta scolded us for disturbing her neighbors. However, Justice ignored her, so I did, too.

"You're so slow!" I teased as I placed my few bags on the kitchen counter.

"You're so weak!" he countered as he littered his much larger haul on the kitchen floor. "I would have beaten you back if you could carry more."

"All part of my plan," I said with a wink as we went into the living room and collapsed on the sofa in front of the TV. Justice tried to headlock me again, but this time I was ready for him and slipped away from his grasp.

"Yeah, you don't want none of this Sid Justice," he boasted as he flexed his biceps. He was built like a bulldog, short and stocky—perfect for his favorite sports, football and boxing. And fake wrestling. His father was an amateur boxer. Everyone in his family was short and stocky like that. I was tall and skinny, and I liked basketball but I wasn't very athletic. I preferred feats of wit.

"Pick up the sticks," I said, tossing the brand new gaming controller at him. It hit his chest and fell into his lap.

"Why?" he asked with a smirk. "So I can kick your ass in Street Fighter again?"

"Say what?" I challenged.

"Did I stutter?"

"Nah," I said, glad to return his smirk. "Not that time." Peeved by my snide remark, he punched me in

9

the side. I tried to anticipate him, but he was too fast. A sudden and sharp pain shot through my ribs. I tried not to let on that I felt it.

"Come on, then!" he said and turned on the console. We started the game, a simulation of martial arts. I won five straight times. He groaned and jumped up to retrieve the boombox from his room. He brought it into the room, plopped back down beside me, and pressed play. The drums and bass filled the room.

"I'm focused, now," he said and picked up the controller again. We played another two rounds. He never landed a hit.

Down, toward, Y.

I missed, so he jumped—as I expected he would.

Toward, down, toward, L.

Uppercut. Critical hit to the chest. His fighter flew through the air and landed with a thud. In frustration, Justice tossed the controller against the console.

"Shit," he said. "See me in a real ring, I bet I'll whoop your ass."

I dropped the controller, too.

"Why you always wanna fight me?" I asked. "You don't like me or something?"

I did not expect his response.

"You kidding?" he said, "I love you. We cousins. Brothers, even."

In truth, we were neither. I was a foster child. Just borrowing his family. I didn't even live in this house. I lived with Mama Etta's daughter, Gloria Rooks, Justice's aunt. His own mother was a dope fiend. His father never lived up to his athletic potential. He became a dope fiend, too. They both passed away in a dope house somewhere. So, Justice lived with Mama Etta. We had that in common, not living with our parents. My father was dead. Lord only knows where my mother was. They were both too young to have me, and my mother gave me up when my father died. I was six years old then. She said that it would only be for a summer. That was eight years ago. Justice was the only people I had. Justice's words did not always match his actions, but I had grown used to him doing things in his own way. I understood him. I suppose in that way, I was the only people he had, too.

"So of course I love you," he continued. "Don't you see me being all happy when you get here?"

"Yeah."

"That's why Aunt Gloria is always sending you over here."

"Yeah," I said, "So why you always wanna fight me, then?"

"I just be playing with you," Justice replied. "You don't like being over here?"

"Yeah," I said as I stared at his shiny new gaming console. I didn't have one at my house. Didn't have a boombox like he did, either, the kind with the equalizers on the front. Gloria said that I would just play the devil's music if I had a cassette player. So, she wouldn't buy me one. She also wouldn't buy me Jordan sneakers. Justice had a new pair, white with black patent leather.

Phat

That's what the boys in the hood said when he walked outside wearing those shoes. No one said the same thing about my Champions. That's cool, though. I didn't do what Justice did to get shoes like those.

"Yo," Justice snapped his fingers as he looked down at the glowing green light on his pager. "L-let's go to the bodega and get something to eat," he said.

"Ain't Mama Etta cooking something?" I asked. I could smell the chicken frying and collards simmering in the kitchen. Biscuits would be on soon. Maybe some Nilla Wafer pudding, too.

"She cooking for later," Justice said. "I'm hungry now. I'mma get some ch-chips or something."

He jumped up and headed toward his room.

"Come on," he said.

"I ain't got no money."

"Don't worry about that. I got you."

I followed him to his room where he took a cloth-wrapped bundle from his dresser drawer and tucked it into his waistband. Then I followed him to the front door.

"We'll be back, Mama Etta," he called out.

"Where y'all going?" she called back.

"T-to the store."

"Boy, I just bought all these groceries for…"

But Justice was already rushing through the door and pulling me along with him. I could hear Mama Etta shouting at us from the other side of the door, but her voice faded to nothing as we hustled down the hall and out the heavy exit door of the building.

Outside, the sun was already setting, and the streets were slowly coming to life. Daytime was always deceptively quiet around here. The sun shone. The birds chirped. The breeze rustled through trees that lined the streets of brick tenements. In the daytime, anyone who didn't live here might have assumed this to be a quaint and peaceful place to live. Anyone who lived here knew better. The quietness was a facade. Hell slumbered in those brick tenements. Rarely did it come outside in the daytime, and when it did, it was really sneaky about it. Hell had a certain respect for grandmas shuffling back and forth to church and school teachers running weekend programs at the libraries. So, hell did things real quietly in the daytime. Or else, it slept and waited for night. As Justice and I left Mama Etta's apartment, night was chasing the sun below the horizon.

"If the demons get ahold of me and I should die," Justice mumbled the rap lyrics to his favorite song, "I wasn't even happy here, so you ain't gotta cry."

I didn't like most rap music. I didn't always identify with the acts mentioned in those lyrics. But sometimes when Justice sang, I felt that I understood the sentiment.

"Where we going?" I asked.

"What you mean?" Justice replied.

"We really headed to the store?" I asked.

"W-we going that way, ain't we?"

"Sure." I said, choosing to break the string of questions even though I knew we weren't going to the store. After all, Justice had stuttered on the way out the door. He used to stutter real bad when we were kids. He had gotten better as we became teenagers, but I noticed that his stutter came back from time to time. He stuttered when he was nervous. Or afraid. Or angry. He stuttered when he lied. I never told him what I knew about his stutter. I figured it gave me an advantage over him.

I wasn't wrong. We walked right past DeJesus's bodega and we kept walking until we approached the basketball courts at the edge of Woodland Park. Here was another place that was more hood than haven. Sure, there were basketball courts and the remnants of a swing set that had been rusted into the earth beneath it, and sure the park had a natural splendor to it: the tall trees, immense grasses, and wild flowers invited the undiscerning eye on imaginings of leisurely strolls. To the discerning eye, however, those trees, grasses, and flowers were riddled with weeds, unkempt brush, and poison ivy. To the discerning eye, this natural splendor held places to hide and places to be hidden. There were only two reasons anyone ever came to Woodland Park, and when I looked again at Justice's shoes, I knew we weren't there to play ball.

"Yo, Twan!" Justice shouted out to a tall, slim guy standing near the courts and watching a pickup game. Antwan Rooks was Justice's real cousin. He wore designer jeans and Timberland boots. He pulled the hoodie up on his black, goose-feather jacket.

Bubblegoose.

That's what we called those jackets.

Phat. Expensive.

I definitely couldn't have one.

"Whaddup, son?" Twan called back as we entered the park. His voice was much deeper. He had a fresh haircut and a thin goatee. He was eighteen. Grown-ass man. Had a car and everything.

"Ice Cold!" he said. Twan called Justice "Just Ice" or "Ice Cold" or usually just "Ice." I didn't like any of those names. Whenever Twan called him those names, I was reminded that he and Justice were real cousins. When they were together, Twan talked to me as if everything

14

was an inside joke that I couldn't get. *Ice* was in on the joke, so I preferred *Justice*.

"What's good, Twan?" Justice asked, bumping fists with Twan.

"Shit, I can't call it," Twan replied. With his tongue, he shifted a toothpick from one side of his mouth to the other. "Just tryna get this paper. I see you brought your offy-ass cousin with you." Twan offered his fist to me. Left fist. I wasn't in the streets like that, but I knew you didn't fist bump with the left hand.

"He your cousin, too," Justice said, pushing Twan's hand away. "Besides, Ace is cool."

Justice called me "Stacey." *Ice* called me "Ace." Sure, Ace was the cooler part of my name, but it wasn't the whole thing. I preferred my whole name; my father gave it to me. Named me after the jazz pianist. Jazz was my thing. Much more than rap.

"I'm just playin' around," Twan said. Then he turned to me. "You know that, right Ace?"

His lips cracked into a sly grin.

Cheshire Cat-ass face.

"Be cool," Justice interrupted. "Twan, you paged me?"

"Yeah," said Twan.

"So, where they at?" Justice asked.

Twan nodded towards the woods behind him and beyond the basketball courts. Justice and I both looked away to those woods, the largest stretch of nature in an otherwise concrete jungle. The sun was long gone, and the mass of trees had become an ominous silhouette against the twilight sky.

"Cool," Justice said.

"This is the test," Twan warned. "Don't get played. If they try something funny, play it cool and come back to get me."

"Won't be no need for that," Justice said as he reached for the cloth-wrapped bundle at his waist. From it, he revealed a large roll of bills. I caught a glimpse of something else, but he tucked the bundle before I could make out what it was.

"Chill here," he said to me. "I'll be back. Then we'll play a quick game and head home for some of that food Mama Etta got for us."

"Where are you going?" I asked Justice.

"Don't worry, li'l man," Twan said.

"I ain't little," I glared at Twan. We were nearly eye to eye with each other. I was tall for my age. Skinny as hell, though.

"Ice," Twan said, "You need to stop bringing this offy-ass dude with you. He weak!"

"I ain't weak," I replied. Twan smirked.

"Look," Justice said. "Y'all sit here and figure out how to be family. I'll be back."

"Don't get in no trouble," I said.

"Ain't no trouble, Ace. You just be ready to run when I get back."

"But we ain't got no ball," I said as Justice headed toward the woods.

"Take theirs," he called over his shoulder. I looked to the guys playing a full court game. They were all older and bigger.

"Yeah, right," I said under my breath. I turned to watch the game, but I could feel Twan staring at me. I anticipated more of his jests, but they never came.

Instead, he surprised me with a compliment.

"You good people," he said. "I like how you got Ice's back and all that."

I didn't reply but continued to watch the game. A player caught a rebound and they all sprinted to the opposite basket.

"I wish I had a brother like you looking out for me when I was your age," Twan continued, "but tell me something: why you gotta be all goodie-goodie and all that?"

"I ain't," I replied.

"Yeah right," Twan remarked. "I be hearing about you getting good grades and all that. Staying out of trouble and all that."

"Where you hear about me?"

"Ice. He talk about you all the time."

"Word?"

"Word. You a smart dude. You can make that work to your advantage. Know what I'm saying? Get you some fresh gear. Stop wearing them wack-ass kicks you be wearing."

"Your aunt got me these for my birthday," I replied without taking my eyes off the game.

"Shoot!" one of the players shouted. The player with the ball did a pump fake and passed to his teammate who dribbled to an open spot and picked up the ball.

"No disrespect to Aunt Gloria," Twan said before he leaned closer to me to speak in a more hushed tone. "But dig, you and me both know she got more bread than that. You don't think she got enough to get you better gear?"

"Shoot!" shouted another player. The guy with the

ball jumped and took a shot. It hit the back of the rim and fell into the hands of the opposing player.

"Listen," Twan said, "I don't knock nobody's hustle, but that foster care shit is just that: a hustle. Aunt Gloria be meaning well and all that, and I know she take care of you. But if you think she ain't holding out on that check that comes for you, you trippin."

"Why are you telling me this?" I asked, finally looking away from the game to raise a brow at Twan.

"I'm just saying, if you ever need some bread, holla at me. I got you."

"Do I have to do what you be having Justice do for you?"

"Hey, Justice is his own man. He don't do nothing he ain't big enough for."

"Shoot!" I heard a voice shout. I looked back to see a player release the ball. It hit the back of the rim once and bounced straight up. Then, as it fell through the net, two cracks of thunder boomed in the park. I watched as no one caught the ball. It rolled away from the basket and toward me, but all of the players were hurrying in different directions. I looked at Twan who was looking off to where Justice had gone. A grin spread across his face.

Cheshire Cat…

A sound like fireworks popped in the woods and when I looked there, Twan started running, too. He didn't warn me. Just started running. Soon, I saw Justice sprinting toward me. I looked down at the ball, which had rolled to a stop at my feet. *Justice* had wanted me to get it so we could play. But, *Ice* was running toward me to grab my arm.

"The ball," I said as he reached me and pulled me away.

"Forget that shit!" he said. Everything after that became a blur. We ran as fast as we could away from the woods and into the streets. More popping sounds like firecrackers rattled behind us. Tires screeched in front of us. A glass window shattered. A motorcycle whizzed by. A lady screamed as we narrowly avoided being hit by a passing bus.

When the world slowed down to normal speed again, we were in the familiar hallway of an apartment building, but we weren't home. We stopped before a door and Justice knocked on it. It opened to reveal the prettiest face.

Sherelle

I used to steal glimpses of that face in elementary school. She was in my class for three straight years before we were assigned to different middle schools. Then we were freshmen in high school, but she wasn't in any of my classes. I saw her in the lunchroom sometimes but never spoke to her. I suppose I had almost gotten over her until she was right there in front of me. My eyes became glued to her.

"Y'all heard them gunshots?" Sherelle asked with wide eyes.

"Yeah, that's why we ran in here," Justice said. "Can we come in?"

"My mama and papa ain't home," she rebuffed him.

"So you gonna leave us out here?" Justice asked.

Sherelle looked down at her bare toes and rocked back and forth for a long moment in the doorway. I looked down, too.

Pretty toes.

Finally, with a resigned sigh, she stepped aside. Justice rushed in. I stood in the hallway and stared. Sherelle noticed me looking at her toes.

"Boy, you's an offy! Hurry up and get in here. You letting the air out."

I grew flush and cleared my throat though I had nothing to say. She walked away from the open door, and I followed her inside.

"Y'all want something to drink," Sherelle asked when we were in the living room. Justice sat down on the sofa and rested his feet on the coffee table. Sherelle nudged them off with her bare legs.

Daisy dukes. Pretty brown legs. Shiny with baby oil.

"I don't know what you do in your house, but we don't put our feet on tables in here," she said.

"Water," I uttered, clearing my throat again.

"I got iced tea," she replied.

"Water is good," I said.

"Give me some of that iced tea," Justice said. When Sherelle went into the kitchen, Justice pulled me down to the sofa. He was oddly excited.

"Wanna see something?" he asked.

"What?"

He reached for his waistband and removed the bundle, which he unwrapped to reveal a revolver. He placed the gun in my hands, and I felt that the barrel was hot.

"What the hell is this?" I hissed, looking up to see if Sherelle was returning.

"You don't know what that is?" Justice chuckled.

"I mean, I know what it is, but why you got it? Did

you—"

"Shh!" Justice hissed. I quieted to a whisper.

"Was that you who fired them shots in the park?"

"Not just me. I fired first. But, don't worry about that. Just hold on to this heat until things cool down a bit."

"Did you kill someone with it? What am I supposed to do with it?"

"Keep it. It's yours," Justice said coolly. "Because the next time you hear gun shots and you reach for a basketball, I'mma kick the dog shit out of you." He replaced the rag around it and pushed it into my lap.

"I don't want—" I began, but Sherelle had returned with our drinks. She placed them on the coasters atop the coffee table, and I fumbled to conceal the revolver in the rag.

"What's that?" she asked.

"Nothing," Justice said, jumping up and placing his arm around her shoulders. "Why don't you show me around."

"Ain't much to see," Sherelle replied.

"Well it'll all be new to me on account of you ain't never let me in the house before."

"That's because my father don't like me having boys over."

"I figure he'll make an exception for me. Come on, show me around."

"I told you, ain't much to see."

But Justice was already leading her down the hall.

"Show me your room, then."

"I definitely ain't supposed to have boys in my room."

"You ain't about to have no boy in your room."

Their voices trailed down the hall and around the

corner. Then her door closed. I unwrapped the gun and stared at it for a moment. Then I wrapped it again and tucked it into my waistband.

Shit.

DEAD AND GONE

Brea and I met sophomore year because she passed me a note in English class one day:

U Justice cuzzo right? She wrote. *Give him my # 860-555-0143.*

I turned Brea's note over and wrote my reply.

You like my cousin?

I dunno. he qt, she replied.

Pandas r cute. Still bears, tho.

She snickered. The teacher glared at her. I scribbled another note on a torn corner of notebook paper.

U r qt.

I looked at the note for a long time before I balled it up and stuck it in my pocket. The bell rang, and she walked over to me.

"So, you gonna give him my number?" she asked.

"Yeah."

She smiled. "K, thanks!"

I don't know why I gave Justice her number. I could have lost it or said I did. I could have told her Justice was too nervous on account of his stutter even though he hadn't stuttered in years. I could have lied. I should have.

"My nigga, Ace!" Justice said when he read the crumpled slip of paper. He was on the passenger side of a convertible BMW. I had jumped in the backseat. Twan was driving. A cloud wafted about the cabin in spite of the convertible roof being down. Music blared from the speakers.

Hail Mary.

Another dark rap song. Only Justice's excitement lightened the mood.

"I been wanting her number all semester," Justice said with a broad grin. "But it's always hard to tell with them smart chicks. Sometimes they want a thug like me. Sometimes they want a nerd like Ace."

"Nah," Twan interjected as he exhaled a cloud from the blunt he was smoking. "Smart girls always want a thug. They got songs about that shit. That's all you right there, Ice."

"Yeah, you right," Justice said, reaching for the blunt. "But if the good girls *and* the bad girls want niggas like me, how we gonna ever get my mans hooked up back there."

Twan chuckled. "Ace'll be alright as soon as he stops acting so wack."

"He ain't wack," Justice said, passing the blunt back to him. "He just did me a solid. He's good."

"Yeah, too good," Twan remarked.

"He just be listening to too much of that gospel my aunt be playing in the house all the time," Justice explained.

"I don't be listening to that," I said.

"He needs to hit this," Twan said, waving the blunt

around before taking a pull.

"Nah, I'm good," I muttered.

"Gospel?" Twan asked as he exhaled another cloud.

"Ain't nothing wrong with praising the Lord," Justice said. He looked back at me. "You be praising Him, don't you?"

"I don't listen to that," I said.

"I be praising Him, too—just in my own way," Justice said.

"Yo, I don't be listening to that!" I said more firmly.

"Ok. My bad," Justice said. Twan chuckled again.

"What you be listening to, then?" Twan asked.

"Lots of stuff," I replied.

"Like what?" Twan asked.

"Big, Nas, Pac—"

"You don't like no damn Pac," Justice interrupted. "That's my music. You listen to Choppin' and shit like that."

"Chopin. And I only play that on the piano," I said.

"Showpaahn," Twan mocked me. "Bougie-ass dude."

"Ace plays the piano," Justice explained to Twan.

"No shit?" Twan replied. "Like Stevie Wonder? Wait, are you blind, Ace?

"I ain't blind," I replied.

"All this time!" Twan crooned. "I never knew. I was thinking you was just goofy, coming up in here just handing over fine bitches' numbers and all that. Now, a guy like me? I woulda kept that little hot tamale's number. But all this time, you been blind. You ain't even know how fine she was. My bad, playa."

"He don't play no Stevie Wonder," Justice said.

"Yo, Stevaaay!" Twan yelled, erupting into a fit of

laughter. "How many fingers I'm holding up?" Justice took the blunt from him and punched his shoulder.

"Don't listen to him, Ace," Justice said, turning in his seat to face me. "You just do you. By the way, you still got that piece I gave you?"

"What piece?"

"The gun I gave you at Sherrelle's place."

"A year ago?" I said. I remembered that gun. I swore the barrel was still hot even a day later. I tucked it away in a hole I had found in my closet ceiling, and I tried to forget about it. Since then, I had dreamt often of that gun barrel growing so hot that it burned the whole house down.

"Never mind," Justice said. "Take this one."

I nearly jumped out of my skin when I saw the revolver Justice held. It was completely identical to the last one. Or, Justice had conjured it from my nightmares.

"What I need that for?" I asked.

"He ain't ready," Twan said.

"Ready for what?" I asked.

"He ready," Justice said.

"He can't shoot no gun," Twan said. "He probably don't even know how to hold it."

"I don't wanna shoot no gun," I said.

"Look," Justice said, "You ain't gotta shoot nobody with it. We just tryna scare him a bit."

"Who?" I said.

"Some dude on the South End—been running his mouth," Twan said. "We just gonna give him a little warning."

"So why I gotta do it?" I asked.

"You don't," Twan agreed. "I told Ice we should just

drop you off at home. But he's convinced you're one of us. I tried to tell him to leave Aunt Gloria's foster son alone, but…"

"Nah," Justice interrupted, locking eyes with me. "Ain't no foster kid here. This is my brother."

I held Justice's gaze. My eyes watered a bit. I hated myself for that.

"So what I gotta do?" I asked.

"All you gotta do is point it," Justice said. "He'll know we mean business. Then we can get up out of there."

I took the gun. It seemed heavier than the one he gave me before, but I was surprised by how calm I was as I held it. Like Justice had been that day. He killed somebody in that park, and then it was like it had never happened. We had gone home and eaten with Mama Etta. Then we played video games. Then we slept. Like normal teenage boys.

"So," Justice said, "you gonna hold us down?"

"I ain't gotta shoot nobody?" I confirmed.

"Nah."

"Then we going home?"

"Mos def."

I looked at him and then at Twan's reflection in the center rearview mirror. He looked back. His expression was earnest.

"Fine," I said.

Justice shifted into his seat again and turned the music up.

"He's good," Justice said.

"I heard 'em," Twan replied.

Justice looked away, out the passenger window. I looked out mine, too, seeing everything that passed just a split second after Justice saw it. We rode the rest of the way silently. There was only the sound of the engine and the wind. And the music.

You really wanna ride or die?

Our destination was a corner store on the South End, just one small, brick building painted white. There was a wooden sign hanging above the entrance.

Casares's Grocery

The words were hand-stenciled in white with a blue outline. The door was wide open. There was one car, a red Honda Civic parked on the side of the building, away from the four parking spaces of the lot. We parked in one of the spaces. As I looked out the window, I saw that this neighborhood was like ours. Silent. Sedated. Sunny.

"You want something?" Justice asked as he got out of the car.

"Hot fries," I replied.

"Then bring your ass inside and get some," he said with his usual cocky grin. I hopped out, feeling the weight of the gun in my waistband.

The bell above the door chimed when we entered. The lights inside were dimmer than the light outside.

"Yo, Casares!" Twan called out before my eyes could adjust. "What up, papi? Papiiii chuloooo! Como estas, my amigo? Donde esta la biblioteca?"

"Who you?" the cashier asked. I guessed he was Casares. As my eyes adjusted to the dimly-lit store, I saw that he was an older man, mid-twenties maybe. Definitely didn't look like a thug. I saw him take a step back from the register. In fact, I noticed everything he did. He frowned nervously. Then, he chewed on his lower lip.

Antsy.

"I'm your amigo," Twan continued. "You don't remember me? Yo Ice, remind this chulo who I be."

"You don't remember my mans?" Justice chimed in. "Two months ago. Summertime. You was hanging out near Woodland Park. You don't remember that?"

"I don't go up there," the cashier replied nervously.

"Come on, papi," Twan said. "You been up there plenty times. Heard you been talking a lot of shit."

Casares's eyebrows rose.

"I don't want no trouble," he said.

"Nah, ain't no trouble, papi," Twan replied. "We just wanna tax you a bit." Twan nodded to Justice who nudged me. They both gave me a knowing glance. I pulled the revolver from my waistband and aimed it at the cashier.

"Hey, hey! Take it easy," the cashier said. "You gonna shoot me?"

"Nah," Twan said coolly, "It ain't like that. I'm on some Gandhi shit today. Just figured you might wanna make a donation, seeing as your people tore some stuff up on our end. Make it right, and we ain't got no problems."

"I don't know what you're talking about," the cashier said looking to Justice and then to me. Then he looked back at Twan.

"Oh, you want money?" Casares asked.

"Exactly, papi. I'm thinking two g's."

"That's it?" Casares said, trying to look relieved.

"Yeah," said Twan. "Real reasonable, right?"

"Muy," Casares replied. "Let me just..." He reached

for the register.

"Yo, hold up!" Justice said. "Ace, watch this dude. I think he got a gun."

"No, no gun," the cashier said nervously, raising his hands.

"Yeah," Twan said, "I think he tryna pull a fast one. Yo, let loose one time on this *goya*. Let him know we ain't playin' with him."

Goya. That word had become a slur in our neighborhood. Puerto ricans ate Goya-brand beans. So, we called them "goyas."

"Let loose?" I asked.

"Shoot!" Justice clarified.

I clutched the gun handle to steady my hand.

"Come on, son," the cashier said to me, when he saw the gun tremble. His hands began to drop slowly. "You just a kid. You ain't gotta do nothing like this."

"Ain't no kids in here," Justice said. "Go ahead and test him."

I looked at Justice, and he nodded. I looked back to the cashier. For a long moment, he stood still. No. He wasn't still. His hands were moving ever-so-slowly. Down, down. To the register. Below the register. To the...

BOOM!

I aimed the gun right, closed my eyes, and fired a shot that whizzed by his ear and destroyed a carton of cigarettes behind him. I opened my eyes to see bits of tobacco and paper fluttering everywhere.

"Ugh!" the cashier groaned, stumbling backwards and clapping has hands over his ears.

"Oh shit!" Justin cackled.

"Yeah!" Twan declared. "You thought we was playing, huh? Get my money!"

"D-dios!," the cashier stammered as he struggled to catch his breath. He felt all over his chest for a hole, and not finding one, looked incredulously at Twan and me.

"My money, papi!" Twan shouted.

"I don't got that kind of money in the register."

What had been a scowl on Twan's face contorted into a smile.

Cheshire...

"That's cool, papi," he said. "I didn't think you did. Just give me some of them cigarillos and we straight."

The cashier didn't move. Twan gestured to Justice to retrieve the goods, and Justice jumped over the counter and grabbed the shotgun that hung beneath the register. Then he stuffed a pack of cigarettes, a few cigarillos, and a handful of penny candies into his pocket before leaping back over the counter.

"This'll do," Justice said. "Lucky my mans ain't smoke you, papi."

I lowered the gun and we hustled out of the store. Twan and Justice laughed. I followed them in a daze.

"What I tell you?" Justice shouted as we climbed back into the convertible. "Cuzzo came correct, didn't he? What I tell you?"

"Yeah," Twan said looking back at me. "Yeah, he held it down. I can't even lie. Took long enough, though. Any longer and we woulda been cremated all over that store." He looked amused, but for the first time, there was also something like admiration in his eyes. I did not want it.

"Who was that?" I asked.

"Nobody," Twan said cooly as he lit one of the stolen

cigarettes and started the car.

"Nobody?" I cried.

"I just needed to see how you'd handle yourself," Twan said. "I knew you wouldn't shoot nobody. Didn't even think you'd pull the trigger."

"Don't tell me nothing 'bout my cuz Ace!" Justice continued to boast. "That nigga is cold. Almost took that goya's head clean off. How that feel? You ready to go home now, nigga?"

"Nobody?" I cried again.

"You woulda preferred it was somebody?" Twan asked.

"I could've killed him," I huffed, my heart beating through my chest.

"No you couldn't've," Twan said. "You ain't no killa like that."

I glared at him through the mirror. He did not look back.

"You big mad, huh?" Twan asked, exhaling blue smoke.

"Look," Justice said to me, "nobody got hurt, and you showed everybody in this car that you ain't no bitch. *And* you fired your first gun. Tell me that didn't feel good. That power?"

I looked down at the gun. I was tempted to agree.

"Right?" Justice said. "You feel it."

I did, but I didn't want to. I shoved the gun into his hands.

"Let's go home," I said. Justice took the gun.

"Ok," he said.

"Get me some hot fries on the way, though," I added. Justice smiled earnestly. He misunderstood my antipathy for affinity.

"You heard him," Justice said to Twan. "Get this nigga some hot fries on the way."

"And a Sprite," I said.

"And a Sprite!" Justice echoed. "My nigga, Ace! Ice Cold Ace!"

The corners of my brow and mouth twitched with the urge to scowl, but I repressed that urge.

Don't let them see. They don't deserve to see what they did to you.

I spent the rest of the weekend trying to be myself, again, but there is nothing harder than pretending to be yourself when you're not. I felt betrayed, and that betrayal had changed me somehow. I was actually grateful when Gloria came to get me on Sunday, even if she was particularly strict after she had been to church.

"You missed some chores on Friday," she told me on the ride home, "so you better do those before you touch that piano."

"Sure," I said.

Even God rested on Sunday. But not me. Not if I forgot my chores on Friday. I was relieved when I could finally settle before the upright piano that we kept in the living room.

Scherzo. Number two.

I was only allowed to play gospel songs in the house. Or classical, if I could find a way to learn it. I did not know if I liked Chopin. I only knew that it wasn't gospel. It was the only thing I knew that wasn't gospel. Or jazz. I wasn't allowed to play jazz in the house. However, each time I finished with Chopin, I paused to hear the jazz in the silence. My fingers even floated over the keys like the ghosts of each note. In this way, I sometimes imagined that my father played alongside me.

Caden Bishop, my father, was a jazz pianist, so I knew jazz before I knew how to speak. As early as I could remember, I learned the notes with him. I used to make wishes on those notes.

Caden was a good man. That's all I remembered about him, all I wanted to believe. He smiled a lot, and he played the piano for me. Used to play for the church, too. He wasn't a religious man, but they let him play in the church. They hoped he would see the light some day, but all he ever saw in there was the music. Outside of the church, he used to run the streets. That's what they told me—sold drugs and all that. But the man I remembered was a good man. Until he got shot. Then he was nothing.

My mother took care of me for as long as she could afford to, which wasn't long at all. She gave me up one month before my sixth birthday. She said she'd come back for me, but she never did. I was alone then, a solitary Bishop in a house of Rooks. No family photos or stories. No family legacy. My father used to tell me of my great, great grandfather who long ago escaped slavery and my great grandmother who was one of the few negro composers of her time.

Blood of a slave. Heart of a king.

That's what my father used to say about my ancestors and me.

Bullshit. A slave can't be no king.

That's what I thought as I sat before the piano keys trying to recall moments when my father played Thelonius for me. I wanted to be that good. But I had started too late. Most pianists start training when they're three or four years old. I had never trained. Only what my father taught me before he died. Then there were things I taught myself along the way.

I played the scherzo once more. Then, when it was late enough and I thought Gloria was sleep, I softly plucked out a few forbidden notes.

'Round Midnight

"That ain't no Christian music," Gloria warned from the top of the stairs.

It damn sure wasn't.

MIDDLE OF THE NIGHT

The first time Brea heard me play the piano was at the high school talent show during our senior year. I was a little older. A lot taller. A bit more of myself: confident and quick-witted. And talented. I won the show that year by playing my own rendition of a song by Stevie Wonder. I even transposed it myself.

Knocks me off my feet...

I did not know that I played it for Brea until I saw her afterward and saw the look of admiration in her eyes. I must have realized then that I had coveted this look from her. We were good friends, though. And, she and Justice were pretty serious. A whole two years and all that. They were both supposed to be at my recital that night. He wasn't. In fact, none of the Rooks were there. Just Brea. I knew they weren't coming. I even knew where Justice was. Brea didn't.

"Did he tell you where he was gonna be?" Brea asked me once the spell of the piano had worn off.

"He said he was going to be here," I lied. I had gotten used to doing more of that, too. Mostly when I was covering for Justice.

"You think he's in trouble?"

"Nah. Not Justice. He can take care of himself."

"That don't mean he ain't in trouble. He just be finding it sometimes."

I placed a sympathetic hand on her shoulder. She looked up at me. I became aware of how tall I was. My hands were bigger, too. That helped with the piano. When I placed my other hand on her other shoulder, I felt strong before her, like I could shelter her from a storm. Or something worse. However when she placed her hands softly upon mine, I thought that I would fall away into a million pieces. I was unsettled by that feeling, so I let my hands fall from her shoulders. She did not seem to notice the change.

"Call him," she said.

"He isn't home," I replied. "If he could be at home, he would be here instead."

"You believe that?"

"I know that. He must've lost track of time somewhere with Twan."

"And you're okay with that?" she asked.

"He has heard me play before. He didn't miss anything."

"Well, you should call him anyway," Brea said with pleading eyes.

"And say what to him?" I asked.

"I don't know," she said. "Tell him to get his ass over here. He'll listen to you. You're a good influence."

I snorted derisively.

"You think I influence him?" I asked. "He doesn't seem any different than when we were kids. He was

37

fully-formed when he was born, and he has been the same ever since. Probably walked when he was born."

Brea laughed more musically then the notes in my song.

"You brought him to me, though," she said.

"That's all?" I said. "I thought you said I was a *good* influence?" She punched me playfully. It hurt anyway.

"You know I bring out the good in people," she said turning away to leave the auditorium. "I'm like magic."

"Magic ain't always used for good," I replied.

She rolled her eyes.

We entered the school parking lot and I walked her to her car.

"You think he's home?" she asked.

"Ok, now we're repeating ourselves," I stated. "You can take me over there to check, but if he's not there, I'm fine to have you chauffeur me around until we end up back here."

"No," she said despondently. Then my leg vibrated against the car door. I took my pager from my pocket and looked at the display screen.

Green light. Justice's number. 911.

"I gotta get home," I said to Brea.

"Is that Justice?" she asked.

"No!" I replied. "Look, I'll call him when I get home. If he picks up, I'll let him know you're gonna kill him."

"I'm gonna kill him so bad!" she said with a slight pout of her lips. I couldn't help but notice her lipgloss in the light of the parking lot lamps.

Strawberry lips

They might have been a weakness of mine if I weren't just her friend.

"Stay good," I said as I rushed off toward home. When I was out of her sight, I turned away from home and toward the gas station. Inside the station, I bought sunflower seeds and used the change for the payphone nearby.

"Where you at?" I asked when I heard Justice's voice on the other end.

"Where *you* at?" he replied.

"Near the crib. Brea's pissed at you."

"She's always pissed about something. Look, me and Twan gonna come scoop you in about five. Change your clothes—you know, dress to impress and all that."

"I can't go in the house right now. If I go in, I stay in. I can't just be out all the time like you."

"Just tell Aunt Gloria you're with us."

"Then I definitely wouldn't be allowed out," I said. "Where we going, anyway?"

"You'll see."

"Just come scoop me from the Exxon up the street. I've lied enough for one night."

"Heh. Aight, cool."

I hung up and opened the sunflower seeds. I placed a handful in my mouth and chewed everything, shells and all. I definitely preferred the shells to the seeds. The shells had all the flavor. By the time I swallowed the second mouthful, Twan and Justice had arrived.

New BMW. Same tinted windows. Same convertible roof.

The music rumbled through the parking lot before the doors were even open. Justice was in the passenger seat. I climbed in the seat behind him.

"Check it out," Justice said, lifting his sleeve to reveal a cross tattooed on his shoulder.

"How you get that?" I asked, hinting at his not having turned eighteen just yet.

"Money talks," he replied.

"Yeah, and bullshit walks," I rebutted. "How they let your baby faced-ass in the seat?"

"Hey, we can't all have beards, old nigga," Twan quipped.

"Don't get mad because your girls be looking at me, now," I said.

"Whatever," Justice said. "Where we're going, all kind of girls gonna be there."

"Yeah? And where is that?" I asked.

"You'll see," Justice said. "My bad for not getting to the talent show. Twan and I was handling some business. You know I woulda been there if I coulda."

"Don't sweat it," I said. "But like I said, Brea is pissed."

"She'll be aight."

We turned onto the main avenue and drove straight for half an hour. Before long, the hood was far behind us. Only trees. And darkness.

"Yo, where we at?"

"Nowhere," Twan chuckled.

"Boonies," Justice said as he occupied himself with the splitting of a cigar. He spilled its contents and scattered them out the window. Then he replaced them with a more fragrant leaf.

"You got heat?" Justice asked me.

"You know I don't smoke."

"Nah, I mean a piece."

"Offy-ass nigga," Twan tried to mutter under his breath. I heard him anyway.

"Man, shut up," I told him. Then, to Justice, I asked, "Do I need one?"

"Nah," Justice replied coolly as he lit the Frankenstein cigar. "I just figured this was one of those 'better to have it and not need it' kind of situations."

I thought about the gun in the ceiling of my closet. I hadn't even looked at it in years. Luckily, I hadn't had to handle one since that incident with the cashier. From that moment, Twan and Justice mostly left me out of their affairs. So, I was surprised that Justice asked me about a gun that night.

"You know the only gun I'd have is one you gave me," I remarked. "Where are we going, again?"

Justice took several draws from the blunt and expelled a white cloud that streamed out the window and faded to black.

"Close that window," Twan said. "You letting all the good stuff out."

"You gonna hit this with us one time?" Justice asked, offering the cigar to me. "Everybody out there is gonna be baked. Might as well fit in."

"I'm good."

"You sure? You're gonna stand out enough as it is."

"I'm good," I repeated. I looked out the window, straining my eyes for a glimpse of something, anything, in that darkness. We passed a solitary house on a hill. Then another. Soon, we were in a neighborhood. Not a hood.

"Turn that music down," Twan said to Justice.

We drove on in silence. Past several large, rather extravagant homes. We took several turns onto darker and more secluded streets. Then we entered the

41

driveway of a large, brick house. We took the winding path until we could hear the music of a rather lively house party.

"You usually bring guns to a party?" I asked warily.

"Only when I'm about to make a little money," Justice said winking at me. "A little insurance policy." We parked behind a cluster of Jeeps and coupes. There was one silver Mercedes at the front, before the garage door.

"Don't forget the stuff," Twan reminded Justice, who opened the glove compartment and removed a bundle wrapped in a paper bag. I lingered in the backseat long enough for Twan to notice.

"You not trying to get into this party?" Twan asked with a sly grin. "I mean, who can resist a free party?"

"Y'all ain't about to have me shoot nobody at a party, are you?"

Twan roared with laughter.

"Bring your simple ass!"

I got out of the car and followed them up the driveway. Justice whistled as we walked by the Mercedes.

"Look at that Benzo!" he said. "Gotta get me one of them when I get my license."

"Go ahead and get one, now," Twan joked. "You in the showroom! These white folks'd just buy another one."

"Nah. I want mine clean. Maybe after tonight."

We walked around the cars and toward the back of the house. The music grew louder. Then there was a light that flickered and illuminated the back lawn. As we approached the back porch, I paused. There were five people sitting out there. They were holding bottles and smoking cigarettes. They were all white. I did not know

42

why that unsettled me, but it did.

Justice and Twan continued on without hesitation.

"What's going on, dudes?" Justice called out to them.

"Alright!" one of the guys, a blond, said as he stood up and came down to greet us. "The party's here, fellas!"

I stopped several paces behind Twan and Justice to listen and watch.

"You got the stuff?" the blond asked.

"Right here!" Justice said. "You got the dough?"

"Always," the blond replied.

"Wait!" Twan shouted, "But do you got the brewskis and bitches?"

"Inside!"

"Hell yeah!" they all shouted as they laughed and gave each other high-fives.

I don't know if I was more wary of this unfamiliar circumstance or the unfamiliar demeanor that Justice and Twan used with them. Either way, I would have to be summoned before I took another step.

"Yo Ace!" Twan called. "Party is going on over here."

Fueled by curiosity more than anything, I continued toward the group. The blond approached me first.

"Ace?" he asked me, extending his hand. "I'm Mikey. That's Matt over there. Johnny with the Sox cap. Luke. Jimbo, like 'jumbo.' You already know which one he is." He called to them. "Hey fellas! Come down here and meet Ace. Make him feel comfortable. Mi casa is su casa, right? We got brewskis in the fridge. Jello shots. I'm sure there's some Jagermeister in there somewhere. That'll put some hair on your chest. You probably don't need it, though right?"

I had never been more conscious of my own face.

43

And he keeps talking. Enthusiasm. Maybe too much.

Justice was more amused than I had ever seen him. There was a glint of facetiousness in his eye. Or perhaps he was just high. I figured I would play along. Twan was already talking to some blond chick by the door. I looked down at the brown paper bag in Justice's hands as he raised it and waved it at Mikey. This was clearly a reminder of something.

"Oh, yeah," Mikey said. "Let's handle the business, first." He gestured for Justice and me to come inside. I was not prepared for what awaited me there.

Light, sunrise eyes and a crown of golden curls. She can't even be real—

"Yo, Ace," Justice interrupted my thoughts. "I'mma go upstairs and handle this business real quick. Get comfortable."

I nodded, but I never took my eyes off her. Justice followed my gaze. When he saw her, he grinned knowingly.

"She fine, ain't she?" he said. "She mixed. Father's white. Mother's from Ghana or Belize or some shit like that. You should go talk to her. She ain't been around black folks in weeks.

"What does that—"

But Justice was already taking the stairs two at a time to follow Mikey. I took only a step toward her before I was surrounded by more chatter than I had ever experienced before.

"Hi!" two girls chimed together as they stepped into my path.

Blonde hair blue eyes. Brown hair green eyes.

"You're tall," said green eyes. "Do you play

44

basketball?"

"Are you here with Justice?" asked blue eyes.

"Uh, yeah," I replied, somewhat taken aback by their directness.

"He's cool, huh?" said green eyes.

"I guess," I said.

"I love his hair," said blue eyes.

"Shut up!" said green eyes. "You're not supposed to talk about their hair. They hate that shit." Green eyes turned to me.

"Sorry," said green eyes. "My friend is stupid. I'm Vicki."

"And I'm—" began blue eyes, but Vicki interrupted her.

"She's stupid. Like I said. Just call her 'Stupid.'"

"And she's rude. Just call her—"

"Whatever!" Green eyes interrupted again. She giggled. I almost burst out laughing.

"I'm Heather."

Okay. They seem nice.

"You don't have a drink, yet," Heather observed.

"Or a name," said Vicki.

"He's quiet," Heather said, "Let's call him—"

"Stacey," I interrupted.

"Staaaceeey!" they crooned.

"That's such a cute name!" Vicki said.

"Adorable," Heather agreed taking my hand. "Well Stacey, you should have a beer in this hand."

"And another in this one," Vicki said as she took the other hand and they guided me into the kitchen. I looked back in the direction of the golden-haired mulatto girl, but she was no longer there.

45

There were clusters of people throughout the house. They were all about my age, so I figured this was one of those MTV-type high school parties. I had never been to one before and I stood awestruck by the strangeness of it all.

Green mohawk. Pink pigtails. Vans. Black lipstick and nail polish. Spiked collar. Vans. Jeans that flare at the bottom and go straight to the ground. Torn jeans. Vans. Torn sweater. Some of the ugliest black combat boots I've ever seen. More Vans.

We were definitely not in the city anymore. The music was strange, too.

Bullet with butterfly wings…

Such a somber vibe for a party. Yet, people were dancing. If you'd call it that. One couple moved at a pace more appropriate for the song's tempo. They made out in the doorway.

"Get a room!" Heather cried as she pushed us past them and toward the refrigerator. She opened it and pressed a cold can into my hands.

"Whaddup, Homie G!" a guy with a buzzcut and a #45 Chicago Bulls jersey said as he offered me a high-five.

Heather and Vicki tried to pull me away from him, but he followed us into the living room and toward the sofa.

"Homie G?" I asked. "Who's that?"

"You!" he said, his hand still suspended in the air, a smile plastered across his face. "Homie G in the hood!"

"Do I know you?"

"You should!" he said. "I'm the coolest mo-fo in this piece."

Bloodshot red eyes. High as a kite.

"You're an idiot, Forrest!" Vicki said. "'Homie' means 'friend.' Stacey is not your friend."

"Yeah," Heather agreed. "He's ours."

"That's just because he doesn't know me yet," Forrest replied. He turned to me and lowered his hand. "Hey, you know how I got my name?"

"Forrest?" I asked.

"'Cuz I got them trees, son," he said before erupting into a high-pitched cackle.

"Go find some potheads, loser," Vicki said snootily.

"Whatever, bitches," Forrest said. "You know where to find me." He grabbed a beer from the fridge and fake-limped into the next room.

"Don't mind him," Vicki said. "He thinks he's black."

"I don't think he's ever been out of town," Heather said.

"I don't think he's ever been out of this neighborhood," Vicki said.

They ushered me into the living room where they pushed me onto the sofa and sat on either side of me. They continued their chatter, and I finished a can of beer while I listened. Then I looked up and saw her.

Hair like spun gold pulled up into a crown of tight curls. Almond skin. Chocolate freckles. Scarlet dress.

The two girls spoke on either side of me, but I no longer heard a word they said. I stood up and walked away from them. Toward her. I hardly even noticed the other people in her group. And I was never more sure of my words.

"I've been looking for you," I said.

"Yeah?" she asked. "Do we know each other?"

"Not yet. But we should. In fact, you should apologize

to me."

She raised a solitary, perfectly plucked brow.

"Oh yeah?" she said.

"For breaking my heart."

"Really?"

"Yeah, it's been skipping all night since I first noticed you."

She looked down at her shoes, but she smiled. Then she shifted her weight from one hip to the other and tucked a loose ringlet of hair behind her ear as she looked at me.

"When did you notice me?" she asked.

"As soon as I walked through the door."

"Why didn't you say something to me then?"

"You seemed too good to be true. I had to be sure you weren't just a figment of my imagination."

She smiled. I smiled.

"I'm Christine," she said, offering me her hand. I took it in mine.

"Ace," I said.

"That your real name?"

"It's real enough."

"But I'm just a figment...?"

"I'll let you know when my heart starts again."

"And when will that be?"

I looked into the non-existent distance and feigned the stillness of a statue. She laughed and I jerked suddenly back to life.

"Where are you from?" she asked.

"The city."

"Well, you need to come to the boondocks more often."

"I think I will."

"They listen to a lot of Smashing Pumpkins in the city?"

"I don't know what that is," I said wryly. She laughed again.

"Get me something to drink," she said, taking me by the wrist and guiding me back to the kitchen. Forrest came in with a large bottle and Christine took it from him. He protested, but she was charming. He didn't stand a chance.

Fireball. Like the candy. Sweet.

"You want some?" Christine asked, pouring some in a red plastic cup.

"I thought I was getting *you* the drink," I said.

"I'll forgive you this time," she replied. She handed me the cup and poured another. "But only if you can dance."

"To this?"

"To anything."

"A little."

"Show me."

She led me into the room where the music was loudest. I took a large gulp from my cup before she stopped close to me. Then she pressed against me and we swayed slowly back and forth.

Sugar and fire

We danced, and the earth danced with us. Her soft curls caressed my chin.

"You forgive me, now?" I asked.

"Yes. But only because I broke your heart. Does it feel better, yet?"

I felt the heat from the Fireball making its way down

my chest. I therefore felt particularly clever.

"Keep dancing with me like that, and it may never beat again," I remarked.

"Wouldn't that be a shame?" she replied.

I took another sip of Fireball. She turned around and leaned back against me, her head tilted back upon my chest.

Sugar and fire

We danced, but the earth danced faster. I felt as though I were on a merry-go-round. She turned to face me again. She stood on her tip-toes to kiss me. The taste of our drinks swirled in my mouth.

Sugar and fire

We danced, and the earth out-danced us. We stumbled and felt silly, so we lay on the sofa. We kissed some more. She rested her head on my chest. I wanted to be still, but the earth still danced. And heaven came down to join it. I closed my eyes for what I thought was the briefest of moments, but when I opened them, the music had stopped and more people were lying on chairs and sofas and on the floor. Christine slept beside me, her eyes closed, her hand resting on my chest. Justice was tapping me on my shoulder. He gestured to Christine.

"That's your girl now?" he smirked. I looked up to see that the earth still danced, and he along with it. "You about to smash?" he asked.

"What?" I groaned.

"*Smash*, son," Justice reiterated. "Can't ask for a better opportunity."

I looked at Christine. Her eyes were closed. She looked like a porcelain doll.

"But, she's passed out," I said.

"Exactly!" Justice said, licking his lips and rubbing his hands. "So, like I said. Is you about to smash?"

"Nah, man," I said, sitting up and rubbing my eyes.

"Let's raise up outta here, then."

I nudged Christine.

"Hey," I said. She raised her head and opened her eyes. She remembered me. She smiled.

"Hey you," she said.

"Let me get your number," I said. "Me and Justice have to go."

She looked over to Justice. She smiled.

"I didn't know you were here," she said.

"I been here the whole time," I replied confusedly. "But I gotta go."

"You coming back?" she asked.

"To the boonies?" I asked.

"To me."

"Most definitely," I said. "But, I can call you in the meantime."

"Ok," she said, resting her head on my chest again.

"So?" I asked. She was quiet. "I can get that number?" She was quiet, still.

"Yo, she bent," Justice said. "Let's get up outta here before my aunt start trippin'."

"What time is it?" I asked.

"Two in the morning."

"Shit."

Outside, I could not feel the cold air, but I knew it was there. The world was silent. The earth still danced. I opened the rear door of Twan's car and collapsed into the seat. On the drive home, I drifted in and out of sleep. Each time I awoke, I had the unsettling realization that time never moves backward.

"I shoulda got her number," I mumbled.

"Shoulda," Twan echoed.

"I'mma be sick," I muttered.

"I'd be sick, too if I had let a fine bitch like that go without getting her number," Twan chuckled.

"Nah," I said. "I'm really gonna be sick!"

"Oh shit," Justice said. "Stop the car."

"Oh hell no!" Twan shouted. Both, he and Justice helped me out of the car. I stumbled to the side of the road and heaved.

All fire. No sugar. Jesus!

I stumbled back to the car where Twan and Justice were laughing.

"We know what his poison is now, don't we?" Twan jested as I climbed into the rear seat again. Justice returned to the passenger seat and looked back at me. I gazed at the orange glow of his blunt before it faded to black.

"You gonna be aight?" he asked.

"Yeah," I replied. Just drop me off a few blocks from the house. I gotta sneak in."

"I got you," he said.

Fade to black

When I opened my eyes, Twan and Justice were trying to stand me up against the car. I shrugged them off and stumbled the two blocks home.

Gotta be stealthy

I paused before the front door. I heaved in the hydrangea bush beside it. When I stood upright again, I noticed that all of the windows were dark. I figured it was safe to enter. I was too unsettled to think better of that choice. Inside, Gloria's rocking chair creaked in the darkness.

Squeak. Creak. Squeak. Creak.

"How was the recital?" she asked, her stern voice cutting through the darkness.

"It was good."

"Good."

Squeak. Creak. Squeak. Creak.

"So—" I began.

"Go on upstairs," she said calmly. "We got church in the morning."

"But it's Saturday," I said.

Squeak. Creak. Squeak. Creak.

I climbed the stairs to my room and lay down. My head fell heavily upon the pillow.

Fade to black

DEVIL IN A GOLD CROWN

So I punched him. Punched Twan. Right in the jaw. Broke it and loosed three teeth from his mouth. Broke my hand, too. It probably wouldn't have happened if I hadn't been at the church that day. But I was. And I saw what I saw.

When I awoke the morning after coming home drunk, Gloria told me that I had the devil in me. I did not believe her. I liked to think that there was a lot of light in me, a light that I had been holding onto since I became her ward and my mother told me she was coming back. She hadn't come. Yet. And, I still believed that I could hold onto that light. Until I broke Twan's jaw. Who knows? Maybe the devil had been in me all along. Or maybe it jumped into me that day. When I saw what I saw.

Gloria did not chastise me on that Saturday. She simply brought me to the church and told me to help out Eula Mae Reeves. That was her cure for the devil: chores. There were floors that needed mopping, pews that needed dusting, and hedges that needed clipping.

In addition to giving out hugs and peppermints, Eula Mae often hung around the church to help handle its business and keep it clean. That day, she oversaw my work, and somehow she made the day tolerable. Delightful even.

"Boys will do what boys do, won't they?" she said. "I know you must feel awful."

"For what I put Gloria through?" I asked.

"No, for what you put yourself through," Eula Mae replied. "I used to go to a party or two in my day. Doesn't feel too good the next morning, does it?"

I smiled sheepishly.

"Come on," she said, "I'll fix you some tea."

We did the tea first. Then the mopping. Then the dusting. Wiping down every pew and choir bench in the church was a tedious task. I was grateful for the company.

"I hear that you play the piano," she said.

"Where'd you hear that?" I asked.

"Sister Gloria. Says you had a recital last night. Says you're pretty good, too."

"She wouldn't know. She wasn't there."

"She hears you practice, though, doesn't she?"

"Not everything. I'm not allowed to play most things in the house."

"Like what?" she asked.

"Basically anything that ain't Christian music."

"Come again?" she said.

"I can't play anything that ain't—,"

"*Ain't?*" she interrupted me again. "Child, you know you're too smart to be saying words like 'ain't.' You don't have to put on that act in here. I know better."

55

I never gave much thought to the way I spoke. I suppose I spoke one way to my teachers and another way to my friends. Eula Mae was signifying that she was not one of my friends.

"Go on," she said. "You were talking about the piano?"

"Yeah," I said. "Mostly classical when Gloria is home. Jazz when she isn't. Mostly I just practice in the music room at school."

"No gospel?" she asked.

"I don't like gospel much."

"What do you like?"

"Jazz. Classical sometimes."

"Want to play something for me?"

"Now?"

She gestured toward the piano in the choir section.

"At church? What should I play?" I asked.

"The Lord doesn't care what you play," she replied, "so long as it's joyful."

I looked at the piano. Perhaps there was a longing in my gaze because Eula Mae walked over to me, gently placed her hand on my back, and guided me to the piano bench. I sat down and lifted the cover to the keys. Then, I placed my hands lightly upon them and played a song my father used to play before I slept.

Lullaby of the leaves...

Eula Mae walked over to a choir bench and sat there with her eyes closed and a serene expression. When I played the last note, it lingered in the air and rose to the high ceilings of the church before it faded to silence. Eula Mae took a deep and satisfied breath.

"That ain't the devil," she said to me. "That's God in

you. So much God." As she said this, I did not expect a solitary tear to trickle down my cheek. I was surprised when a few more fell. Then I was overwhelmed by a torrent of them. I did not know where they came from. But, Eula Mae seemed to know because she didn't even look surprised. She just came over and hugged me. One of those full, bosom-heavy hugs that makes you feel that no evil can touch you.

"That's a gift in you," she said.

"No," I replied, surprised by the anger in my own tone. "It wasn't my gift. It was my father's gift. But, he didn't get to use it."

"Where's he now?"

"Gone."

"No one's ever really gone. He passed his gift on to you. That's part of the blessing."

"Damn that!" I shouted. Those words rose to the high ceilings of the church and lingered up there. However, Eula Mae did not scoff at my reaction. In fact, her expression softened.

"You miss him?" she asked. I would not let myself answer that. It was bad enough that I cried. However, I would lament.

"What kind of blessing is it if someone else has to be cursed for you to have it?" I asked.

"Who said anything about someone being cursed?" Eula Mae asked.

"No one does," I replied. "Everyone talks about being blessed, but if I'm blessed to play the piano, my father must've been cursed to give it up."

"That's not how blessings and curses work," she said.

"Then how do they work?" I asked. "Because I'd

much rather have him here than the piano."

"Somehow, I don't think you'd give up that music for anything," she replied. "Besides, he lives in you—every song you play."

"That's it?"

"What more do you want?"

"I don't know. But there has to be more."

"Like what? Become some fancy musician? Make a whole lot of money?"

"Maybe," I said.

"Son, you don't need all that material stuff to use your gift. Every time you sit in front of those keys, you revel in it. Every time you play, a little bit of God rings out."

I wiped my face on my sleeves.

"That must be easy for you to say," I replied. "You got all the material stuff."

Eula Mae laughed heartily, "Lord knows that stuff comes and goes. It ain't like what you got." She stood up to leave. "Nope, can't take what you got away from you, but the taxman sure enough takes what I have. All the time, all day long."

"Do you think I can come here and play some time?"

"You can come here and play for me any Saturday you want," Eula Mae smiled. "It won't trouble Sister Gloria for you to be here. She thinks you have the devil in you. She doesn't know any better."

"Jazz?" I asked.

"As long as it's joyful." Eula Mae patted my shoulder and rose to leave down the aisle, between the pews, and out the large wooden doors. When my hands returned to the keys, I played the piano solo to a song by Mary Lou Williams.

The Devil rests not in morning, nor midday, nor midnight...

That was the closest thing to gospel that I could play. But it was still jazz, an unsettling song that somehow soothed my soul. When I played the last note, I headed outdoors to trim the hedges by the church gate. That's when I saw what I saw.

A black BMW approached the cross section in front of the church. The convertible top was down. On the passenger side, I saw a flash of golden curls. I remembered their softness against my chin. I dropped the hedge clippers and scowled as I walked toward the stopped car at the traffic light. I wanted to be sure that they knew I could see them, but before I could get there, the light turned green and they sped away. I saw her. She did not see me. He did. And he sneered.

That night, I was supposed to stay with Justice. Gloria did not want me in her house.

"If you're drinking, now, maybe you're too grown for this house," she had said. So I went to Mama Etta's house after I finished up at the church. But when I got there, I lingered in the doorway, watching Justice who appeared to be on his way out.

"Did Twan come home with us last night?" I asked.

"How else do you think we got home?" Justice replied. "You must've been more drunk than you looked. And you looked pretty messed up."

"Do you know where he is?" I asked.

"Somewhere minding his business probably," Justice replied. "Why don't you call him?"

"Nah," I said. "You're probably right."

However, I did not budge from the doorway.

"You gonna come in?"

"I'm good," I replied. I noticed that Justice had his jacket on.

"Where are you going?" I asked.

"I'm going t-to mind my business, too," Justice replied.

"Cool," I said. We stared at each other a moment longer before I turned back to the door. "I'm gonna go see Twan."

"W-wait. What? Now? What if he ain't home?"

"I'll wait for him."

"W-what's wrong? Why do you need to go over there unannounced?"

"I need to ask him something."

I opened the door and walked through it.

"Wait," Justice said. "We'll go together."

"I don't need you to come with me," I said.

"Yeah, you do. You look mad. I don't know what you mad about but when I'm not around, you and Twan don't know how to act right."

Twan's place was close enough to be in the same town but far enough to warrant a bus ride. When we arrived there, I did not take for granted that it was different from the party in the boondocks the night before. I recognized the clothes and the movements. I understood the beats in the music. There was no welcoming party. Just a kid about my age who was collecting a cover charge. Even the alcohol was different. King Cobra. Crown Royal. Majestic shit. Same red cups, though.

Justice and I made our way through the smoky, crowded hallway. There were a few faces I recognized. Some were from school. Most were from the block. Others were strangers to me, and almost all were older. Among them, I was looking for two particular people, and I didn't see either of them. Justice and I entered the living room and saw Sherelle and Brea talking with some guy by the window. I didn't recognize the guy. Neither did Justice. He charged over there, and I forgot my own objective for a moment.

"Who this?" he asked as he placed his arm around Brea.

"Who you?" the guy replied.

Wrong answer.

Justice huffed, but Brea calmed him.

"You don't know Sherelle's boyfriend?" she asked. "He's from the south end."

"Oh, you be eatin' them Goya beans," Justice snorted. The guy's chest swelled and he tightened his fist.

"He's just playing, Lucas," Sherelle said. But, Lucas took a step toward Justice. He was bigger and taller, but Justice stood his ground. "Hey," Sherelle said, stepping between them and placing her hand lightly on Luca's chin to direct his gaze to hers. "Get me a drink." Lucas's expression softened, and the blood in his chest ebbed. They walked away toward the kitchen, and Sherelle jabbed Justice's forehead with her index finger as she passed him. "Stupid boy!" she grumbled.

"Why you always like that?" Brea scolded him when the two were gone.

"I ain't like how he was looking at you," Justice replied, only a little bit remorseful.

"With his girl right there?" said Brea.

"That don't be meaning nothing with some of these dudes," Justice said.

With the crisis averted, I let their words fade into the background and returned to my mission.

"I'mma get a drink," I said to no one in particular.

I walked into the kitchen and filled a red cup with Crown Royal.

"You don't want no juice or nothing in that?" said someone whose face I was already forgetting. I didn't respond. I took a gulp from the cup and felt the burn settle into my chest. I walked away to the dining room where I found my targets. They did not see me. I took another gulp and approached slowly. Raising the cup to my lips, I sipped a bit more and gained more courage with each step. When I arrived within an arm's length of them, Twan noticed me. He exhaled a cloud of smoke. His eyes were red and droopy. I looked at Christine. She looked drowsy. She did not seem to remember me.

Shit. I don't remember you neither, then.

"Hey, little nigga," Twan said drowsily as he put out his left fist to greet me. "Hey! Y'all say hello to my foster cousin." I lowered my empty cup.

I guess I have had enough.

And then I punched him, swung my right fist as hard as I could into that Cheshire-cat face of his. I heard the crunch of bone on bone. On bone. On bone. Louder than the music. Louder than the scream let loose from the mulatto girl or the yelp from my cousin. Louder than the goons who swarmed me afterward. They pulled me away from Twan. One of them punched me in the gut. I coughed up a bit of courage on him. Something solid struck me in the head. That pain was dulled by the satisfaction I got from watching Twan attempt to curse at me. I looked at him and sneered because his jaw would not let him put the words together. Then Justice entered the room. His mouth fell open. I must have broken his jaw, too.

"What the hell happened?" Justice shouted as someone grabbed me around the waist and slung me into a wall.

"Yo, you gotta get him outta here," another voice said.

"Yo, stick that ni—," said a much angrier voice. But, Justice came and pulled me away from the swarm just as the blade of a knife flashed in the chaos of scattering girls and menacing guys. The earth spun and danced around me as Justice and I made our way down the hallway and out the door.

"W-w-what the hell did you do?" Justice screamed as we reached the sidewalk outside. We ran several blocks until we arrived at the park. When we got to the basketball courts, Justice stopped me.

"W-w-what were you thinking?" he asked as we caught our breaths. "What did he do to you?"

"I think I broke my hand," I said.

"That ain't all you b-b-broke," Justice said. "W-w-we're both going to hell, now. C-c-come on."

We crossed the street and headed toward his house.

Hell. I guess there is a bit of the devil in me.

I looked down at my hand.

Won't be no God shining through anytime soon.

A FISTFUL OF DARKNESS

My father used to tell me that there was no heaven or hell. Just earth and men. Earth can be heaven or hell. It all depends on what men are willing to make of it.

"So hold on to that light," I said to Eula Mae as we sat at the piano in the church. "That's what my father told me. 'Hold tight to it. Because it's so much easier to get ahold of darkness if you're not careful.' He used to make me practice holding on to light." I stopped to smile at the memory. "'Go ahead,' he used to say. 'Try it. Reach out into that daylight and try to grab hold of it. Close your hands tight around it. Now peek into those fists. What do you see?' Of course he knew what I was going to see every time."

"Clever man," Eula Mae said. "And what did you see in your fists before you hit that boy?" We both looked down at the cast I had been wearing for the past month.

"Whole lotta darkness," I said.

"Mhmm," she agreed.

We were both quiet for a moment before I spoke

again.

"She didn't have to put me out the house, though," I lamented.

"Sister Gloria will come around," Eula Mae replied. "But you gotta show her you can do better. She kept you close, didn't she?"

"What do you mean?"

"Her mother is taking you in. She could have called up one of the group homes after you broke her nephew's jaw."

"She did!" I cried. "It was Justice who insisted I stay with Mama Etta and him. Gloria was glad to get rid of me. Is that what a mother is supposed to do?"

"If she's trying to teach a lesson, sure."

"No." I shook my head. "She doesn't care. Besides, those checks will be drying up soon. She'll be glad to be rid of me."

"That's what you think?" she asked.

"That's what I know." I said.

She shook her head sympathetically.

"So, you're staying with your cousin and grandma for the summer," Eula Mae said, hoping to lighten the mood. "Could be fun."

"Mama Etta is too old to be a grandma," I replied. "Grandmas are supposed to have rules, but ever since Justice and I were thirteen, she has pretty much let us do whatever we want. At this point, it's more like she's living with him than the other way around."

"Could be *really* fun, then," Eula Mae joked.

"Yeah, Justice knows all about fun," I remarked.

"So some good came of it."

I didn't reply. Instead, I gazed at the black keys of the

piano before me.

"Well," she sighed, "Go ahead. Play something."

I placed my good hand on the keys and hammered out a few notes. The lefthand side of jazz always sounds the most brooding. Eula Mae laughed.

"Yeah, that's darkness alright," she said. "So how else can you cure the devil? There aren't many chores left around here, and you can't play me a song."

I shrugged.

"Can you paint?" she asked.

"Like, a picture?"

"No, a wall," she said. "At my place. I have a bathroom wall that needs painting."

"I've done some painting before," I said.

"Good. Let's do that, then. If you're lucky I might even feed you. How does that sound?"

"Sounds good."

I followed her out of the church. As we approached her car, I noticed that it was even nicer than I had imagined.

Red Mercedes. Leather. Wood trim.

We got in the car and she fidgeted a moment with the fancy key before starting the car. When we exited the church parking lot, we drove in silence; she did not play music in the car.

"So, who was the girl?" she asked after we had driven awhile.

"Girl?"

"It's usually a girl," she explained, "that gets boys to fighting."

"Nah," I said. "Wasn't no girl."

"Sure. But you have a girlfriend?" she asked.

"Yeah, I mean no," I uttered, "I mean I like girls. Girls don't like me, though."

"A tall, handsome young man like yourself?"

Black boys don't blush. Lucky me.

"I imagine you'd be beating them away with a stick. No?"

"No," I replied.

"Well, the right one will come along soon enough."

"Nah, I'm done with that."

"That's a shame. What girl can resist a man with battle scars?" she chuckled.

"A girl that don't want no cripple," I said, tapping my cast against the passenger window. It made up for the silence of the car stereo.

"Does your speech usually suffer when you're angry?" she asked.

"I ain't angry."

She chuckled again. I sighed. We drove a bit farther in silence.

"Families can be hard on us sometimes," Eula Mae said. "Your mama is just trying to raise you the best way she knows how."

"What mama? I only call one person 'mama,'" I said.

"And what does that person call you these days?"

Silence. Tap. Tap.

"A person only has one mom," I replied.

"A person can have as many moms as he wants."

"Well, I only have one mom."

"You could have more."

Silence again. Tap, tap, tap.

"When was the last time you saw your biological mother?" Eula Mae asked.

"I don't know," I replied. "A long time ago."

"What was it your father said about holding on to light?"

"I'll see her again. That's the light."

"And what if you don't?" Eula Mae asked.

"Ain't no light in thinking you'll never see your mother again," I replied. "Especially if she's alive."

"Perhaps," Eula Mae said. "But, how do you know you aren't holding on to darkness?

"What darkness?"

"Spite," Eula Mae explained. "Anger for every year that passes without seeing your mother. Check on those clenched fists of yours. Sometimes hope becomes bitterness when you're not paying attention."

"Is that what you think?" I asked. "That I'm bitter?"

"I think that your father was a wise man. Make sure it's hope you're still holding. Make sure it's light in those fists of yours."

I sighed and tapped my cast lightly against the window. There was something comforting in the vibrations that reached my ears but hardly touched my skin.

"So," Eula Mae began again, "you said that you're *done with that.*"

"Yeah."

"So who was the girl?"

Tap tap tap tap…

"Nobody," I said.

"Tell me about nobody."

"I mean, there *was* this one girl. I think I missed my chance with her, though."

"Go on."

"I don't think I'm her type."

"And what type is that?"

"You know. The bad boy type."

"How bad you wanna be? You wanna break *both* hands?" Eula Mae had a musical laugh. It went well with her hugs and peppermint.

"I don't wanna be bad at all," I said.

"Glad to hear it," Eula Mae said as her laughter faded. "Good girls don't want bad boys anyway. Not the truly good ones. She married?"

I rolled my eyes.

"She's my age," I said.

"Good! You have plenty of time then."

Silence. Tap. Silence. Silence. Tap.

"So you didn't punch the boy over that girl?" Eula Mae asked.

"No. I mean… what?"

"So there's another girl?"

"No, I mean, I wouldn't punch nobody over no girl."

"Anybody," she corrected me.

"Nobody," I reiterated. "Triple negative."

"Mhmm," she hummed—that sound black women make to remind you they know everything.

We drove for about half an hour before we arrived at her house. She lived on the West End. The rich people's end. Where the mansions were. And the white people.

As we walked through the large, oak door, I felt for the first time that I was entering a home. I had lived many years in Gloria's duplex, which was neat and clean enough. Justice and Mama Etta lived in subsidized tenement housing that was just good enough for eating, sleeping, and shitting, as Justice often put it. But, Eula

69

Mae's house was a home, and entering it filled me with a strange sense of hope and dread: hope in the existence of places like this and dread in the notion that I did not belong in them. It seemed that I did not really belong anywhere. So awestruck was I by the look of the high ceilings that stretched toward heaven and the windows that were so wide they seemed to harness the whole sky, I felt like a thief, catching glimpses of things to covet, things that were too far beyond my grasp.

Every room was a place to behold. The living room was adorned with furniture that looked like works of art. The dining room felt like a banquet hall for kings. And the library...

Oh the library!

When I entered it, I felt that the rhythm of my heart was amplified, that the walls echoed my very own song. Thousands of books sat on shelves with glass cabinets. Elegant paintings and statuettes adorned the walls and walking spaces. But, the most beautiful thing of all, in the center of the room, was a beautiful, black, baby grand piano. Perhaps Eula Mae heard my song playing in that room, too, for she guided me into it as she once guided me to the piano in the church. Only, I could not play this piano. I could only look at it. And I looked at it for a long time. And I dreamed.

"Maybe next time," she said after a moment. "Come on. The wall I need you to paint is this way."

It took me a few hours to apply the coats of cornflower blue that Eula Mae wanted, and as we waited for each coat to dry, she showed me the other chambers to this heaven of hers. It was when we walked through the garden that I realized we examined this place alone.

"You were asking about me earlier," I said. "What about you. Were you ever married?"

"For many years," she said with a reminiscing smile. "I suppose that's the light I hold onto, now. You carry your father's music with you. All I have is my engagement ring. But, I try not to carry that anywhere if I can help it." She chuckled.

"No children?" I asked.

"They're all grown, now. My youngest just went away to college. He's hardly older than you. Nope, it's just me in this big house. I suppose I should sell it, but I don't think I could bring myself to do that. Too many things worth holding onto."

"Doesn't it get lonely here by yourself?" I asked.

"I'm starting to get used to it," she said. "Besides, I'm at the church so much, I hardly do much here besides eat and sleep."

"I would do so much more," I said.

"Really? Like what?"

"Like play the piano. Read the books. Or just sit out here and look at the plants and flowers."

"Eventually you'd get lonely."

"I don't think so," I said.

"You would. Trust me. You aren't holding that much darkness."

By early evening, I had applied the final coat of paint to the bathroom wall. We had supper in the garden, and as we returned from it, we passed a stone lantern. It was not lit, but something inside caught the last glint of sun and gleamed just enough for me to discern what it was. I felt more like a thief, then, for I knew that I was not supposed to know what was in that lantern. But, I did.

And, I coveted it. We passed through the glass doors at the rear of the house and walked the long hall to the front door where we exited to the driveway and the red Mercedes.

"You should come by again some time," she suggested as we got into the car.

"You have more work?" I asked.

"I will," she replied. "But come by any time and just say 'hi.'"

"I get my cast off on Monday," I said.

"All the more reason for you to come by," she remarked. "There's a bus that runs up the main avenue a few blocks away."

"Any time?" I asked.

"Any time you need some light," she said.

She drove me all the way back to the North End and as we rode, I watched paradise pass on by. At Justice's place, I dragged my feet all the way from the parking lot to the place that was not my home. Inside, I discovered a tremendous amount of ruckus.

"I don't want this nonsense in my house!" Mama Etta shrieked from her frail throat and lungs as she thumped her bony fists against Justice's bedroom door. On the other side of that door was the source of that nonsense. Walls banged and furniture moved. A girl's voice wailed. A boy's voice railed. Then the door swung open and Justice stormed past Mama Etta, knocking her fragile body against the wall. He looked through me as he reached the front door and passed on through it and down the hall. I looked into the bedroom to see Brea huddled in a corner between the wall and a nightstand. Her hair was tousled, and her sweater was torn.

With Justice gone from the house, Mama Etta muttered something to herself and returned to her room. I, with clenched fists, approached Brea, and she with tear-filled eyes looked away from me. I got close to her, and she let out a blood-curdling cry. Perhaps she meant to deter me from approaching, but I did not heed her. I knelt beside her and lightly touched her hands which were wrapped around her own neck. I had to pry them loose. At first she resisted, but then she let me see what she was hiding.

Black and purple bruises. Light-brown neck and collar bone. So much ugly on so much pretty. So much dark on so much light.

BLACK STARS AND BRIGHT SKIES

felt that I had approached a wilted flower as I knelt before Brea and held her hands in mine. She turned to me with raindrop eyes and lips that quivered like petals in a storm. When she parted those lips to speak, I thought they might be torn away by the words that pushed past them.

"Why is he so awful to me?" she asked.

"Because you are too good to him," I replied. I did not know where those words came from. I did not know what it meant to be good to someone or what it felt like to have someone be too good to me. But those words felt like the right ones to say. I had a sudden desire to touch the bruises on her neck, not to soothe them or cause her pain but simply to wonder if I were capable of leaving such scars on someone. If I could be so jealous. If I could love anything so much yet harm it out of the fear that it would not love me back. I had a desire to touch those bruises because in their darkness were so many things I had never felt before.

She let him do this. She loves him so much that she let herself be the light in his dark fists.

I looked around Justice's bedroom, which looked as though a storm had torn through it. And in the midst of that storm was this bruised and tattered flower.

"You should get up from here," I said. "Leave before he comes back."

"But I can't move," she whimpered. "I cannot walk. I cannot even stand."

"You can," I assured her. "I will help you."

"How?" she cried.

"I will carry you if I have to."

"Carry me where?" She was nearing hysteria. "Where can you carry me that I will not find myself here again? It's like—it's like I'm rooted here."

"You are not," I said. "You are so strong,"

"Am I?"

"Take my hands. I will show you."

She placed her hands firmly in mine, but she did not stand. Instead, she pulled me down to her, and I wrapped my arms around her. She laid her head upon my shoulder, and I saw clearly the marks that spread over her skin like the Milky Way across a night sky, except that the stars and space had switched places.

I pressed my lips against that night sky and she winced. I kissed those black stars once more and at first she did not move. Then suddenly she pulled away from me.

"What are you doing?" she asked.

"I only thought," I stammered, "I mean, I felt I should do something to take the pain away."

"You kissed me," she said, "kissed Justice's girl."

"I'm sorry. I only wanted—"

She pressed her lips against mine and breathed the words from them. I held her closer. Then, as she pulled away, it occurred to me that kisses were misunderstood. It is not the start or even the middle of a kiss that makes it good. The goodness of a kiss is at the end. When the lips fall away from each other like honey dripping from a spoon. And you open your eyes to see hers. And everything is understood.

"How long?" she asked.

"Since always," I replied as I stood up.

"Yeah?"

"Absolutely."

"Then I have been so foolish," she said. I wanted to say something more, something soft and tender. But then I remembered where we were.

"You should get out of here," I said.

She was so strong then. She stood, too. However, she didn't leave. Instead she reached up high to place her hands delicately around my neck, and she stood tall. Taller. Upon the balls of her feet and the tips of her toes. And our lips became like honey pouring onto itself. I felt as light as a dandelion seed. I rose. I was warm. So warm. But the warmth quickly faded, and I was cold. So cold. Ice cold. I had gone too high. Up in space. No air to breathe. No gravity to anchor me. Up, up, away from the ground upon which I had safely stood all my life. I was drifting away. And I was terrified.

I pushed away from her and walked away to the door, and as I reached it, Justice appeared there.

"You're still here?" he looked past me to ask Brea.

"She's leaving," I said.

What had he seen?

"Nah she ain't," Justice said. "Since she's still here, I figure I have a few more things to say about that dude I saw her creepin' with."

"Not tonight," I said. "Tell her tomorrow."

"Nigga, who is you?" Justice snapped. "Her daddy or something?"

"I'm just saying," I replied, "you have had enough of each other."

"Nah, I haven't had nearly enough of her, yet."

"She's leaving!" I declared. Justice looked at me with astonishment at first. Then anger.

"Says who?" he asked.

"Says me," I said. "Let us by."

I stood before him, a full five inches taller. However, I trembled.

"Oh, you a superhero, now?" Justice said, clenching his fists.

"No," I replied. "Just a friend."

"You gonna have to move me from this here door, then."

"No, he won't," Brea said in a clear and firm tone. She had found her strength. "Move out of my way."

This time, Justice directed his astonishment at her. No anger. Just surprise. In fact, he was so surprised that he stepped out of the doorway, and Brea brushed past us to get out of the door. Justice and I both looked at her neck as she left. When she was gone, Justice glared at me.

"You smashed, didn't you?" he asked.

"What?"

"Wrong answer, son."

"Wait, you think I did something with your girl?" I tried to sound incredulous. I don't think I convinced him.

"She was acting real different," he replied.

"Maybe she got tired of getting beat on," I said.

"The hell are you talking about? I-I never hit her."

"Come on, Justice. I heard everything as soon as I walked through the door."

"I don't know w-w-what you're talking about. Must be that other nigga she talking to that left those scars on her."

"She ain't talking to nobody," I said. "She loved you to death."

"What did you just say?"

"That she loves you? You know that."

"No, you said it like it was the past. Is that what she said?"

"No," I said, swallowing hard. "But after the way you treated her today—I mean, do you think she deserves that?"

"Deserves what? I ain't do nothing to her but love her. She ain't never gonna find nobody that loves her like I do. Especially not no bitch-ass nigga like you."

"I ain't no bitch," I muttered.

"No? You a fighter? You a killa? That's what you feel deep down in your heart? Like you could pull the trigger to defend someone you love?"

"I did," I said.

"When? You talking about the store? When you shot a box of cigarettes? You must be crazy. You ain't no killa like that."

"No," I said. "I ain't like you."

"Goddamn right, you aint like me. Bet you wish you were, though."

"Yeah, right."

I turned to leave the room, but he stopped me with words that would stay with me for the rest of the night and all of the next few nights and mornings.

"Stop letting these bitches turn you into Superman," he said. "That ain't you. Besides, all she's doing is using you to get to me. Why else do you think she was still here when I got back?"

I shook my head and left the room. I figured he might follow me out. Put me in a headlock or something like that. But, he didn't. He probably knew that his words did enough damage.

I went to the living room, my temporary bedroom, and lay awake on the sofa most of that night. When I finally dozed off, I dreamt of honey kisses. And black stars in the bright sky.

THE BEHELD AND THE
BEHOLDER

A week passed before I saw Brea again. We met in the park and she laid her head on my shoulder like she usually did. Only, it meant something more that time; I could not help seeing the fading stars on her neck and collarbone. I felt again like a thief coveting that which did not belong to him, but I also felt that she didn't mind being coveted. If she did, she would have covered those scars.

I needed to tell her that I was not her hero. I did not rescue her; I stole her away from Justice like a villain would, in a vulnerable moment when it was easiest to get her from him. And if I had to fight Justice, she would have watched me be broken to pieces. Justice was right. I wasn't a hero. There was no fight in me, and if there were, I wouldn't have used it for a girl. Not again. She needed to know that. I needed to tell her because, she was laying her pretty head upon my shoulder, and it seemed that she felt safe there, secure in my presence.

It was alluring to feel her closeness and imagine myself strong enough to sweep her off of her feet and place her upon a pedestal reserved for only the most beautiful and revered things. I would love her more than she could love herself, for beauty is rarely in the eyes of the beheld. I would love her more than I could love myself, for the beholder of beauty cannot stand on the pedestal with her. The strength of the beholder is supposed to be in his reverence. Yet, I revered her and felt that I had somehow been weakened. As she lay her head upon my shoulder, assured of my chivalry, my bravery and strength, I looked skittishly around the park, terrified of who might see us.

"We can't be together," I told her. She raised her head in alarm.

"Why not?" she asked.

"There'd be no happiness in it," I said.

"How do you know that?"

"Because of Justice."

"Oh," she said, returning her head to my shoulder. "Is that all?"

"I couldn't do that to him," I said.

"I see," she said. We indulged a silent moment before she continued.

"Do you know what I realized when you kissed me?" she asked. "I realized that love feels good. That it's supposed to. Justice said he loved me, but it always hurt."

"That's because he hurts," I said. "All over, he hurts."

"Yes," Brea agreed. "And it's all he knows. It was all I knew, too. But you…"

"…hurt like him," I interrupted. "We've been through the same shit."

"No, you don't," she said. "And no you haven't. I can tell."

"Why? Because of a kiss?" I asked.

"Maybe," she said.

"You needed to be kissed, so I kissed you. That's all."

"I don't even believe that," she said.

"But it's true," I replied. "That's all it can be. Otherwise I'd have to fight my cousin, and I won't do that. He's all I got."

"If he's all you have, then you might as well let it all go," she chuckled. I did not.

"Maybe I already have," I responded. "I try not to want what I can't have."

"How do you know you can't have it if you don't want it?"

"I know that I can't have it. That's why I don't want it."

"That must be a miserable way to go about life."

"It's the way I know," I explained. "When you want things, they can be taken from you."

"It's usually worth the risk, though," she said. Then, she moved defiantly closer so that her entire body rested upon mine. "You can have me. If you wanted to. Truly."

"And Justice?" I said. "Seeing us together would kill him."

"Kill him, then."

"Yeah," I snorted. "I'll do it tomorrow. Right after dinner. Then I'll kiss Mama Etta goodnight."

"Great!" she laughed like a song. "Then you'll be all broken to pieces. Just like Justice. Then I'll be your type."

"Yeah?"

"Yeah," she said. "Only problem is you won't be mine.

Not anymore."

We were both silent then, listening only to the breeze through the improbable trees. I gave in to the allure and the reverence. I decided to want something I couldn't have. So caught up in this notion did I become that I almost missed seeing the BMW that passed in the distance.

A BETRAYAL OF THE HEART

Words don't hurt. Not if you don't let them. The truth certainly doesn't hurt. But even lies cannot pierce the heart when you know the truth behind them. Justice was lying. I knew that. I just needed to know why.

"Th-things have been g-good b-between us," he said. "Sh-she ain't thinking about that no more. N-neither am I. And you know what? You sh-should t-talk to Twan, too."

He hadn't sounded that bad since we were kids. Perhaps his stutter had returned. Or perhaps his tongue was burdened by the truth he buried in the silence between each syllable.

"Why do I care about Twan?" I asked.

"B-because he family," Justice said, "And because you gotta be tired of avoiding him, hiding over there on the west end. Does that old lady even pay you for the work you be doing for her?"

"Sometimes," I replied.

"Sometimes? A rich lady like her?"

"Yeah, sometimes," I said.

"Then what you going over there for?"

"Music," I said. "She let's me play her piano."

"So you do that, too, and you still don't get paid?" said Justice. "I didn't know you were that cheap."

"I ain't," I said. "I like to play. Ain't no piano around here, so…" I trailed off. Justice laughed.

"You need to get right with Twan, then. Get some money and buy your own piano."

"Twan don't wanna talk to me," I said.

"He ain't even m-mad no more," Justice said. "The way he figures it, anyone bold enough to cold-clock him the way you did—with all of his boys right there? That's somebody he wants on his side."

"How's his jaw?" I asked.

"Same as your hand," Justice replied. "You back on that piano. He's back to talking his shit."

"He ain't mad?"

"N-nah. Tr-truthfully, he forgot all about it until I mentioned it to him the other day."

"What did he say?" I asked.

"Nothing. J-just wondering where you been. He thinks you're still mad at him about—well, you know."

I snorted derisively.

"I ain't even thought about her since that day," I said.

"I didn't think so," Justice said. He paused as if he expected me to say something else. I had no other thoughts on the matter.

"You should go see your cousin," Justice continued.

"I will," I said.

"We can go see him tonight."

"Tonight?"

"Yeah," Justice said. "I need to drop something off over on the west end, as a matter of fact. Figured I'd bring you along, get a little paper, and then head over to Twan's after that."

"He's cool with that?" I asked.

"Yeah. And look at it this way: if you can patch things up with him, Aunt Gloria might start to feel better, too.

"Yeah," I said. "So, where are we going?"

"West End," Justice said.

"And I don't have to do anything?"

"Nope. Easy drop off. Y-you don't even need no heat with you."

"Better to have it and not need it—" I said.

"M-man, forget I said that," said Justice. "Maybe that's why things got messed up in the first place: we always tryna get you to act different. That ain't your style, and it don't have to be."

"Yeah," I agreed.

"Them clothes, though," Justice chuckled. I looked down at the old clothing I had worn to cut Eula Mae's lawn. I smiled sheepishly.

"Aight," Justice said. "You change, and I'mma grab the package real quick. Then we can head out."

When Justice went into his bedroom, I searched for better clothes in my suitcase, which I kept behind the sofa that I slept on. When I found what I wanted to wear, I searched further for the gun that Justice had given me so many years ago.

Better to have it…

I tucked it into my waistband and joined Justice in his bedroom where he was preparing a bundle wrapped in a paper bag.

I had a sense of déjà vu, except there was no Mama Etta cooking in the kitchen. Some mornings, she came to sit on the sofa and read the paper. Most days she watched television in her room or napped all day. When we left the house, no matter the hour, there was no rebuke.

Outside, I followed Justice to a familiar black BMW.

"Ain't this Twan's?" I asked.

"It was," Justice explained. "But he has a new whip. This one is mine, now."

I walked toward the passenger side.

"Wanna drive?" Justice asked waving the keys.

"Me?"

"Yeah. I bet you ain't never drove no Beamer before."

He tossed me the keys.

"That old lady be making you drive her around in that Mercedes like *Driving Miss Daisy*, huh?"

I rolled my eyes.

"Nah. She don't let me touch the car."

We climbed in, and I turned the ignition to hear the engine purr to life. Music thumped through the speakers.

Dogs for life...

We cruised down the road. Justice smoked. I felt the effects.

"Turn left up here," Justice said through a cloud.

"Left?" I asked. "Up the Avenue?"

"Yeah."

"Eula Mae lives this way, too," I noted.

"No kidding?"

"What kind of deal we got going on up there?"

Justice inhaled and held the smoke in.

"The rich people kind," he uttered before chuckling

and exhaling a plume that filled the car.

We drove for about half an hour before I realized that Justice had not given me any new directions.

"You s'posed to be the navigator," I said.

"Oh, my bad," Justice said through another chuckle. "I forgot."

"Yeah, weed will do that to you," I quipped.

"Hold on," he said, fumbling around in his pockets. "I got the directions right here somewhere…"

"You at least know the address?" I asked.

"Hold on. Let me check the other pocket."

He fumbled like that for several minutes before he finally gave up.

"Damn, man," he said. I must've left the paper with the address back at the crib."

"So we need to go back?"

"Yeah, man. My bad."

I pulled off to the side of the road and prepared to do a K-turn.

"Hold up," Justice said. "You said your new grandma live out here somewhere, right?"

"Grandma?" I said.

"You know. That old church lady you be hanging with."

"Eula Mae. Yeah, she live out this way."

"Let's stop by. Say 'hi.'"

"She ain't there," I said. "There's a prayer service tonight."

"Oh, word?"

"Word."

"So she ain't home?"

"Nah."

Justice became quiet as he finished his smoke. I completed the turn and began heading toward home.

"Let's go see the house, anyway," Justice said as we sped down the avenue.

"In the dark?" I asked.

"Just a peek," he said. "I ain't never really seen none of them houses on the West End."

"And you won't. It's too dark."

"Come on, man," he pleaded. "It's close, right?"

"Yeah. Off the avenue."

"Real quick, then."

He sounds earnest. He's also high as a kite. I am, too.

"Aight," I said.

I turned the car off the main road and headed toward Eula Mae's house. We arrived minutes later.

"See?" I said. "Can't see a damn thing."

"Let's get a little closer, then."

He jumped out of the car before I could refuse and I turned off the car and followed.

"Yo!" Justice exclaimed. "This is dope!"

"You can't see anything."

"She ain't got no guard dogs or nothing like that, do she?"

"Nah, nothing like that."

He stopped several paces from the front door. There were no lights on, and the silhouette of the house was made bigger by the darkness around it.

"You think we'll ever live in a place like that?"

"I hope," I said. "Some day."

"Let's go inside," Justice said.

"Wait, what?"

"Go inside. I know you have a key."

"I don't have..." I trailed off, remembering the lantern at the back of the house.

"She ain't give you no key?" Justice asked.

"No, but I think I know where she keeps one."

I don't know why I told him that. My knowledge of that key had been with me ever since my first visit. Perhaps I had coveted a chance to enter the house as if it were my own. It would have been like entering a home, someplace to belong. Whatever the case, I found myself leading Justice to the gate that separated the front and back yards. It was Friday and the prayer services usually ran late. I hoped Eula Mae had a lot to pray about.

A FISTFUL OF LIGHT

could hardly see a thing. There was no moon and no stars. No trees nor flowers. No thing of beauty that had once shown itself in the morning sunrise or golden hour. The sun had set long ago. The yard through which Justice and I crept was too far from the street to be touched by the lamps there. The horizon was a void. The night sky bled into the silhouettes of trees and other shadows. Even the house was but a looming presence before us as we crept toward it.

I tried to remember where all the plants were but had to drop to my knees and feel along the ground to where the cobblestone path began. I would have chosen to do so if my toe had not caught one of those cobble stones and sent me stumbling onto the path. Justice stopped behind me.

"You good?" he asked.

"Good enough," I said as the air poured into the tear on my pants and a sting settled into the cuts on my knee. "I found the way. Follow me."

I stood and tapped my foot on the stone ahead of me

to assure myself that I was headed in the right direction. Then I placed my hands out in front of me to search for that gleam I saw on my first visit. I stumbled forward and waved my hands about, certain that though I would not see what I was looking for, I would feel it when it was near.

At last, my hand scraped against the rough, stone structure.

The lantern.

I rubbed my hands against it until I found the opening. Then I found what lay inside, the gleam that I had noticed before but wished I could put out of my mind in that very moment.

A key.

I wrapped my hand around that key and continued forward. The house loomed larger then, and I knew that I had arrived when I could no longer discern the night sky from the silhouette of the home. Things came into focus then, and I reached out with my hands to feel the smooth glass of the back door. I fumbled along that surface until I palmed the doorknob. Then, I slipped the key in and entered. There was a faint beep, but otherwise, all was silent.

"We home, nigga!" Justice said.

"Good," I said. "Now let's go."

"Wait. We just got here."

"And we can't see anything," I said. "Let's go."

I went to tug on his sleeve when a sudden burst of white light beamed in my eyes.

"Can you see now?" Justice said.

"You just happen to have a flashlight with you?" I asked incredulously.

"Better to have and not need, right?"

He began walking around the place picking things up and putting them down again. He placed some crystalline thing in his pocket.

"What are you doing?" I asked.

"Admiring, Ace. Admiring."

"Put that back!"

"What? I didn't even take nothing."

But I saw him take it. He lied. And I couldn't tell that he lied.

I followed him as he went from room to room, picking up items here and there, placing some in a pocket, and putting others back where they did not belong. I tried to return the things he did not steal to their right place. I thought to stop the entire ordeal, but he moved with a furious pace—a sense of urgency.

Soon, he turned toward the stairs, and before I could catch up with him, he was in the master bedroom. When I found him, he had clearly discovered what he was searching for.

On the dresser, before the mirror, was a jewelry box. His eyes were wide as he stared at the largest jewel in the box.

"You see that?" he said, picking the engagement ring from the pile.

"You can't take that," I said. "Her husband gave that to her. He's dead. Put it back."

"Okay, Superman."

He placed it gingerly in his pocket and gently closed the jewelry box.

"We're out of time," he said as he bounded from the room. I stood frozen until he yelled at me.

"Come on!" he shouted from the stairwell. "You wanna get caught?"

I realized then why he was in such a hurry. I ran out the room and down the stairs, chasing him through the house until we had passed through the back door. Justice paused in the yard and listened for a moment.

"Lock the door," he whispered. "I'll be at the car."

When I reached the car, Justice was leaning casually against the driver's door.

"We got about a minute to get the hell out of here before the cops come," he said. "Gimme the keys."

I hesitated.

Our fates are tied.

"Whatever," I said as I tossed him the keys.

We got in the car and sped away. Just as we turned at the main avenue, a police cruiser passed us in the opposite direction.

Justice chuckled as we headed back to the North End.

"You big mad, huh?" he asked.

"You lied to me," I said.

"And you lied to me. Out there messing with my girl. I saw you at the park with her."

"Of course you did," I said calmly. "We always meet there."

"Yeah. I should've stopped it back then, too."

"So we robbed Eula Mae because you think I'm messing with your girl?"

"You *is* messing with my girl."

"Whatever."

"Yeah," Justice said. "It don't matter anyway. She ain't leaving me no how."

"What you mean?"

"Did I stutter? I mean the bitch ain't going nowhere. She gonna be with me. How you feel about *that*?"

"I don't feel no way about it."

"Cool. Then you don't feel no way about how I saw her tonight. Smashed it and everything."

I huffed. I didn't mean to.

"Yeah nigga," Justice said. "You big mad."

We approached our neighborhood and turned on the road at Woodland Park. We usually go straight.

"We going to Twan's?" I asked.

"Y-yeah."

We had both sobered up by then.

"Why we going this way, then?" I asked.

"H-he ain't h-h-home," Justice said. "W-w-we gotta go to his b-b-bitch's crib. Th-this is a sh-sh-shortcut."

We sped up as we cruised down the road. Then we made a sharp left onto a side road, into the natural splendor of Woodland Park. We weren't there to play basketball.

There weren't many street lamps in the park, just enough to keep you on the road. We stopped under one of those lamps. A mist began to fall lightly out there, but somehow I could feel it in my eyes.

"Why you always wanna fight me, man?" I asked.

"I don't," Justice replied somberly. "Get out the car."

"I thought we were family."

"No," Justice said. "Twan is family. The nigga whose jaw you broke? That's my family."

I blinked away the mist. That gave me a certain clarity.

"You right," I said.

"I know," he replied. "Get out the car."

I didn't move.

"Do you remember the day I gave you Brea's number?" I asked.

"Yeah. Why?"

"You lied to me, tricked me into almost shooting an innocent man. Why?"

"Because ain't nobody innocent. Not even you."

"But why him?"

"Why not?"

"You didn't even know him. He ain't do nothing to you."

"Everybody done something wrong," Justice said. "Everybody just don't get caught. Think of that as punishment for something he got away with."

"And who decides the punishment? You?"

"That's up to the universe," Justice said, "I'm just in it. So, yeah. I guess."

"And what if he actually was an innocent person?"

"Like a saint? Nah. Everybody got some dirt on 'em."

"What about you?" I asked.

"You know my dirt."

"Then who's gonna punish you?" I asked.

"I already been punished. You, too. Since we was born. I'm just playing catch up. Get out the car."

I opened the car door and placed one foot onto the black road, already slick with mist. Justice opened his door and we stepped out of the BMW together. The rain began to fall harder.

"Come on," he said.

I walked around to his side of the car and stopped several paces away. He could have shot me then.

"Keep going," he said.

I looked away to the woods, those dark, immense woods.

"You remember when you shot that dude out here?" I asked.

"What are you talking about?"

"Like four or five years ago. I came out here with you and Twan and you shot a dude out here. We were supposed to play basketball. That's what you said. But instead we ended up running for our lives. You remember that?

"What about it?"

"Why did you give me the gun?"

"What?"

"That gun. You shot someone with it and then you gave it to me."

"Yeah, and Twan shot somebody and gave it to me. So what?"

"What was I supposed to do with it?" I asked.

"I really didn't give a damn."

"You want it back?" I asked.

"What?"

I revealed the gun.

"You want it back? Or you gonna use the one you brought?"

"I-I ain't even got one."

"I always know when you're lying," I said, my eyes welling with tears. "Why you always wanna fight me, man?"

For the first time since I had known Justice, he was at a loss for words. He stared slack-jawed at me.

"I-I-I don't," he finally stammered. "I l-l-love—"

I didn't hear the rest of his answer. Only the thunder

of the gun he had given me. A bullet into his chest. A glimpse of light into the darkness. My heart torn apart.

"Sh-shit," he hissed and shook his hands as if they were wet. Or hot. His own gun fell from his waist when he lifted his hands to shake them, and it clattered onto the shimmering asphalt.

"Y-you br-brought it, h-huh?" Justice stammered as he began to shiver. "Y-y-you be listening to m-m-me. W-w-we is f-f-family a-a-ain't we?"

He stumbled a bit and curled slowly to the ground. Like a wilted flower. Erratic breathing and all that. A police siren waled in the distance. It grew close for an instant. Then it faded away. I stood frozen, my hand still aiming the gun.

"I'm-m-m s-s-sorry," he said. "I was j-j-just tr-tr-trying to b-b-be a g-g-g-good cousin. T-Twan told me to be a good c-c-c..."

He struggled to place his hand in his pocket. He fumbled around there for a moment before he pulled his clenched fist out and raised it to me. He opened his fist and revealed Eula Mae's ring. I lowered the gun, then.

"S-s-stacey," Justice clenched his eyes closed. "I d-d-don't wanna d-d-die. D-d-don't let me. W-w-we f-f-f..."

I looked at the ring in his trembling hand. He could not hold onto it much longer. I walked to him and closed my hand around it. Tight. Tighter.

"I'm gonna get you to a hospital," I said.

"W-w-what you gonna t-t-tell 'em?" he asked.

"The truth," I said.

"The tr-tr-truth?" Justice coughed again. He tried to smile but grimaced instead. "Of-f-ffy-ass n-n-ni..."

I knelt beside him and placed my arms under his waist

98

and knees. With all of his strength, he reached up and patted me on the back of the head. Then he hooked his elbow around my neck, and together we strained to get him into the car.

"My h-h-hero, S-stacey," he said, becoming a bit delirious. "W-where we going, s-s-son?"

"Home," I said. I secured him in the backseat and hurried to the driver seat. Then, I drove as fast as I could to the emergency room. I don't remember much besides his drowsy ramblings and the sound of my own heart pounding in my ears. I also don't remember crying out for help, but I do recall the hustling of the nurses to get him from the car and onto a stretcher. As they secured him, Justice looked up at me. He held out his hand and I took it.

"Y-y-ou my c-c-cousin?" he asked.

"Yeah," I said. "Yeah, Justice, I'm your cousin."

"W-w-where you g-g-gonna b-b-b-be at?"

"Right out here. Waiting for you."

They whisked him away, but I did not follow. I couldn't. There was a warm gun in my waistband and a stolen ring in my pocket. I knew that I could only return one.

I stuck my hand in my pocket and closed my fist around the ring.

Finally. A fistful of light.

I turned toward the shimmering street and headed into the rainy night. Alone.

CPSIA information can be obtained
at www.ICGtesting.com
Printed in the USA
FSHW021012170620
70953FS

9 780999 904305